Cole automatically reached for her coat and helped her slip into it.

'You're too kind.'

If only she knew. Cruel to be kind was more like it.

As Lina slipped her arms into the sleeves and shrugged the coat over her shoulders Cole was struck by how fragile her neck looked. Before they'd gone out she'd swept her hair up into some sort of semi-tamed twist. A few tendrils had come loose and were brushing along the length of her neck, her shoulders. It was taking some serious self-control to stop himself from reaching forward and letting the pad of his thumb or the length of his finger draw down the length of her neck. He could just as easily imagine dipping his lips to kiss the bare, pale swoop of skin between her neck and shoulder...

Lina abruptly turned around, their noses nearly colliding. Cole instinctively grabbed hold of her so she could steady herself, but in that moment—and it *was* just a moment—with her face within kissing distance, her eyes catching his, Cole knew he'd have to channel his deepest powers of control or risk everything.

Dear Reader,

I'm so glad you're here! And 'here', this time, is in my semi-adopted town of London. Both Lina and Cole—my hero and heroine—come from other countries and fall in love in London! I can say from experience it is a delight! Then again, falling in love just about anywhere is lovely, isn't it?

Sometimes I struggle with getting the names of my characters just right—but this time I had a double dose of inspiration.

There is a great physiotherapist character who is named after our WHSmith Competition Winner #WHSBookmarks Gemma Holland! It's such a great name, and it was easy to make her character just as fabulous. Gemma, I hope you enjoy your literary incarnation! I have my fingers crossed that this book will delight you.

My second splash of inspiration came from a most excellent friend—Michelle. All I had to do was turn her into a Polish ballerina and *voilà*! Lina Keminsky was born.

I hope you enjoy this journey of healing and new beginnings. Please do feel free to let me know what you think. I love to hear from readers. I can be reached on my website, annieoneilbooks.com, or via Twitter @AnnieONeilBooks.

*Annie O'*Xx

LONDON'S MOST ELIGIBLE DOCTOR

BY
ANNIE O'NEIL

First published in Great Britain 2016
By Mills & Boon, an imprint of HarperCollins*Publishers*
1 London Bridge Street, London, SE1 9GF

Large Print edition 2016

© 2016 Annie O'Neil

ISBN: 978-0-263-26117-2

Printed and bound in Great Britain
by CPI Antony Rowe, Chippenham, Wiltshire

Annie O'Neil spent most of her childhood with her leg draped over the family rocking chair and a book in her hand. Novels, baking and writing too much teenage angst poetry ate up most of her youth. Now Annie splits her time between corralling her husband into helping her with their cows, baking, reading, barrel racing (not really) and spending some very happy hours at her computer, writing.

Books by Annie O'Neil

Mills & Boon Medical Romance

The Surgeon's Christmas Wish
The Firefighter to Heal Her Heart
Doctor...to Duchess?
One Night...with Her Boss

Visit the Author Profile page at millsandboon.co.uk for more titles.

This book is a delight to dedicate!
The heroine—Lina Keminsky—is inspired
by one of my favourite people in the world.
She is kind, passionate, and a most excellent
maker of strawberry daiquiris! Thank
you, Michelle Kem, for being the flame of
creativity behind this flame-haired heroine.

**Praise for
Annie O'Neil**

'A heartwarming tale of two opposites
falling for each other. Annie O'Neil has
done a fabulous job with her first offering.
Highly recommended for readers of medical
romance.'

—*Goodreads* on
The Surgeon's Christmas Wish

'A poignant and enjoyable romance that
held me spellbound from start to finish.
Annie O'Neil writes with plenty of humour,
sensitivity and heart, and she has penned a
compelling tale that will touch your heart and
make you smile as well as shed a tear or two.'

—*CataRomance* on
The Surgeon's Christmas Wish

'A terrific debut novel, and I am counting
down the days until the release of
Annie O'Neil's next medical romance!'

—*CataRomance* on
The Surgeon's Christmas Wish

CHAPTER ONE

IT WAS OFFICIAL. This was Lina's worst ever nightmare in the history of nightmares. Who knew it would have such well-appointed surroundings? En Pointe's reception area was about as Zen and soothing as it got. Creams and sages and tactically placed throw pillows in accent colors just the right side of understated chic. The polar opposite of the way she felt.

Auditioning—no, scratch that—*interviewing* for a job where she'd have to face her demons every day from nine to five? Someone up there was really testing her. Or having a mighty fine belly laugh. If this was her ultimate low, she was well and truly looking forward to the high.

A dark twist of pain tightened in her stomach. She'd had her highs—as a prima ballerina for three glorious, unbelievably wonderful years. Yes, she'd had her highs.

When she'd received the call from her former

dance captain that there was a job going here, her first instinct had been to refuse it. It didn't even sound real to her. Something officey at London's premier dance clinic? That was the *one* job going in the whole of the city? Not that anyone in the ballet owed her anything. Not now.

She scanned the room. Okay. Fair enough. From the lack of a human on Reception she could see it was not a pretend job they'd made up just to get her out of her flat, but *really*? The path from prima ballerina to phone answerer was a bitter pill to swallow and already it felt like she was choking.

"What do you want to rely on? Your good looks?"

The words of her former ballet director—the notorious Madame Tibold—rang in her head. Over and over and over. So, here she was, feeling the opposite of pretty and down-to-the-bottom-of-her-piggy-bank broke. In the interest of keeping her landlord—and the ballet director's haunting words—off her back, she was here. Seeing as she was out of the house she might even see what change she could rustle up for a visit to the Polish deli. A taste of home would be nice. Even if she could only afford a small one.

She looked around the waiting room and felt her face going into scrunched-up *don't want to be here* formation. She fought it and forced her expression to return to *rehearsal hall* neutral. The one that didn't show the pain.

When Lina was really being honest with herself, this job was a lifeline she needed to grab. There wasn't a chance in the world she would call her parents for money after the sacrifices they'd made in her quest to become a ballerina. A small-town teacher shelling out again and again for shoes, tutus, training, trainers, foot stretchers, arch blocks…the list was endless. She owed them her very soul and would never ever ask them for anything again.

The most precious thing she "owned" was her shiny new titanium hip joint, which would have been difficult to hawk, and—more to the point— there would be no more income from the pirouette and plié department from here on out so it was time to look elsewhere. Which turned out to be here—En Pointe—where London's hottest ballerinas came to be fixed. She might as well have left her pride on the coat hook when she'd come in.

But, hey! She was Eastern European. She could take it. Her hand automatically slipped down to massage her bionic hip as yet another nonlimping dancer swept past her out into the hubbub of early evening London. She could always tell dancers apart from…civilians…by their posture and physique. Lucky minx. If she was smart, she'd cherish every single moment she had as a ballerina. *She* certainly had.

All the doctors said she was supposed to have healed from the surgery by now, but she still wasn't a hundred percent. She shook her head, a wry smile playing across her lips as her fingers toyed with her cane. Who was she kidding? She'd never be a hundred percent again and the fear that came with embracing that fact was threatening to destroy her. Just the buzz of the clinic wrapping up a busy day of sewing ballerinas back together for another night onstage—a night she would never have again—was like being seared with a hot poker again and again. No wonder she rarely left her flat these days. The pain that went with it was too much.

"Michalina Keminsky? I'm Dr. Manning."

"Lina," she snapped automatically, before looking up to match the male voice to the man. Uh-oh… She wished she'd not resorted to her post-accident narkiness quite so quickly. She remembered when people used to describe her as the "nice one." From the frazzled look on the man's face, a big load of attitude was the last thing he needed. Not that he didn't look like he could handle it. He was tall. Six-foot-somethin'-somethin'. And fit. Not to mention a healthy dose of straight-up-her-*strasse* good looks, as well. His deep caramel-colored skin spoke to a mixed-race heritage. No stylized hairdo, just a smooth grade two from a not very talented barber, from the looks of things. Her fingers twitched, fighting a curious urge to reach out and run her hands along his head and then see what else happened.

Interesting.

She hadn't felt physically charged in "that department" in quite some time. And his eyes! Two of the bluest, loveliest, darkest-lashed eyes she thought she'd ever seen. An optimum combo of sexy and nice.

"You coming?" He looked up for a nanosecond from the chart he was holding. "I've not got all day."

Okay, fine. Not so nice, then. But at least he spoke in one of those American Southern drawly type accents. It took the edge off. She pushed up from the sofa, trying not to make it too obvious she favored one hip over the other. Even so, false sympathy made her cringe.

"You're the boss."

"Not yet." He shot back. And then smiled. A nice and easy American smile.

Hmm. The jury was still out on this one. Dr. Cole Manning. He had been running En Pointe for a year after a stint up north with a rugby club, so she'd never met him in her prima days. A bit of a nomad, from the sound of things.

From monster athletes to the most delicately tuned ballerinas. Interesting switcheroo. Rumor had it he'd taken over for the clinic's founder, trying to escape some demons of his own back in the US. Then again, the rumor mill in the dance world was about as sharp-tongued and *schadenfreude*-laden as one could get. One dancer down meant another dancer in. After a lifetime of dedication she was now getting the full glory of being the dancer down and it hurt. Big-time.

"After you." Still focused on his chart, Cole gestured that she should head down the corridor before him. Not her favorite position as it would mean he'd probably see her limp. Not that the cane she carried wasn't already a dead giveaway. But she wasn't here for an audition. Only something she'd never done before in her whole entire life: a job interview. Not that she'd bothered to dress up for it or anything. Her thick, out-of-control hair was stuffed into a couple of over-the-shoulder plaits and she hadn't even bothered borrowing something businesslike. Not when she was already perfectly at home in her favorite forest-green swishy rehearsal skirt. Never mind that it had become her favorite swishing-round-the-house skirt. It was still her favorite. And it swished. A girl had to grab her delights where she could.

A smile teased at Cole's lips as "the favor" swooshed past him. He'd heard Lina was still smarting after her hip injury but at least she didn't seem depressed. He believed anger was always better than the bleakness of despair and, from what he'd heard, Lina Keminsky had plenty to be upset about. Anger he could work with. It could be channeled into something productive. Something that made your world come alive again. Experience had taught him that time and again over the past five years. At least he was still able to do what he loved. In Lina's case? She was going to have to do some proper soul searching.

"I've spoken to the City of London Ballet..." He let the words travel along the corridor and saw her spine stiffen, but the speed of her gait remained unchanged. The dance company would've done its bit for her as long as she was on the roster of dancers—but the phone call he'd received from Madame Tibold had confirmed she'd been officially signed off a few weeks ago. It was now seven months since her accident. Long enough to be up and about. Long enough to be facing the truth.

Unexpectedly, Lina whirled round at the end of the corridor, green eyes lit with sparks of passion. "I suppose they told you my performance as Giselle was an excellent career pathway to answering the telephone."

It wasn't often someone took his breath away and this was one of those *Whoa! Howdy! Take a look at what we have here* moments.

So. This woman was the "favor."

Huh. Well. In for a penny…

He went to respond and found himself bereft of words. Peculiar. It wasn't an affliction he usually suffered from. But what sort of human came close to having green eyes so…so *green*? Lina's strawberry blond hair accentuated the extraordinary shade of pale green that—at this particular juncture—was being cloaked by heavy-lidded suspicion. Just like a cat. The way she held her body, tilted her head at him, impatiently tapped her foot—they weren't having the off-putting effect on him they were meant to. Her soft Polish accent just added to the overall affect. Mesmerizing.

There was no mistaking the dancer in her. Even if she'd chosen something else to do, she would command the eye. Lina Keminsky oozed sensuality. And a healthy dose of get-the-hell-out-of-my-business. Which, strangely, made him feel right at home. He knew that feeling, too. It was why he'd thought working with a bunch of rugby players would suit him. A no-feelings zone. Turned out, no matter where he went, those better-off-forgotten memories insisted on clipping at his heels.

No. Lina wasn't emanating serenity—but she had showed up. It was something.

He could easily imagine how beautiful she would look with a smile peeling apart those tightly pursed lips of hers. Even they were a different hue than mere mortal lips. A pale pink rose color. And it was all natural. No lipstick or gloss. Not a speck of makeup anywhere and, from where he was standing, so much the better. Lina pulled the sides of her navy crossover cardigan in more snugly over her front. He'd caught a glimpse of her collarbones as she'd tugged it into place—a bit too prominent, he thought.

"We're looking for someone with your experience." The words were out of his mouth before he could stop them. He hadn't ever actually planned to hire her. Just do the interview. That had been as far with the favor as he'd been prepared to go for the director of City of London Ballet. They had a lot of former dancers on staff, but they couldn't take everyone. Particularly if they weren't willing.

"What experience would that be, then? In breaking their hip, destroying their life, or both?"

"Reception." Which she should've already known.

"And that involves…" Impatience ran across her face.

For heaven's sake! Who was interviewing who here anyway? Despite his best efforts, Cole heard his crisp, officious voice come out. "We need someone capable on Reception. Someone who knows about dancers would be a perk." Depending, of course, upon the level of "perk" Lina would bring to the job.

"I guess that rules me out, then." Lina arched a brow, daring him to contest her.

Cole could feel the urge to rise to the challenge properly awaken within him. This woman didn't want a pushover. She wanted combat.

He turned his own accent up a notch. Having a mother who'd grown up a dyed-in-the-wool Southern belle had its advantages. It had been drilled into him for years. *The impression you make is everything. What you really feel doesn't matter a hoot.*

He gestured to his office door. It was time to get

the balance of this little tête-à-tête back in order. "This isn't normally how I conduct job interviews, Ms. Keminsky, so if you wouldn't mind—"

There was a whimper from a small willow basket just inside the doorway and they both looked down. Puppy was looking up at them with his mournful eyes.

Good thing he wasn't sentimental. The little tricolored ball of fur would already have a name if that were the case. His receptionist—*ex-receptionist*—had called it Fluffy and there was no chance Cole was going to run around the park calling out that name. Not that keeping it—him—was part of the plan. It was temporary. *Right, Puppy?* He gave the mutt a grudging nod of thanks. They could, at the very least, work as a team while they were stuck together.

"Right—so now you see why we need a receptionist."

He pointed at a chair across from his desk and scooped up Puppy's basket at the same time.

"Why?" Lina asked drolly, folding into the chair. "He no longer likes to answer the phones?"

"He's broken his leg so he finds the hours too

long. On top of which he doesn't make a very nice cup of tea," Cole replied.

Lina maintained a neutral expression. She was clearly a woman who didn't fall for corny lines. As if to confirm his theory, she raised a dubious eyebrow at him, then moved her eyes to the puppy.

Interesting. Not someone who cooed straight off the bat. Now, *that* he liked. Not to mention being able to spar verbally with someone. Ballerinas…hmm…

Ballerinas had thick *and* thin skin and it was sometimes impossible to tell which tack to use. Lina definitely didn't seem as though she needed coddling. Quite the opposite, in fact. While she took in his hodgepodge attempt at a puppy carrier—hey, needs must and all that—Cole took another studied look at her.

She was hands-down beautiful. A bit too thin. Proud. Still had a slight limp after the hip surgery, which really shouldn't have been there if she'd been doing all the rehab. And obviously resented being here. To hire or not to hire?

His number one motto sprung to mind: It's up to you. And Lina Keminsky didn't look like a willing player. This wasn't a charity. It was a business.

A frantically busy one even in the quiet times. And with her chip-on-the-shoulder attitude, he didn't know if he could offer her the post. Not without making more work for himself.

"Our receptionist found herself a flamenco dancer who could only get work in Spain. He asked her to elope the same day as she got Puppy here. I guess the lure of the Latin lover won out. All of which is to say there's an urgent need for a receptionist here at the clinic. Comes with a puppy."

Lina's fingers drummed along her collarbone, her expression impassive. She never liked to react to things straight away and she could tell Cole was assessing her. A twitch or a frown spotted by the ballet master could've knocked her off her career path so she had taught herself to smile or remain expressionless, then deal with the fallout in private. Just like she was trying to do right now. Except…

Right now? Right now it was all she could to keep her fingers from dancing the tarantella, let alone keep her pulse in line.

Her stream of visitors since the accident had

gone from steady to trickle to nonexistent. She liked it that way. At least she thought she did.

But a blue-eyed, caramel-skinned and ridiculously long-lashed Dr. Charming, complete with a fluffy puppy in a basket? *Unh-unh.* No. She hadn't banked on that.

She looked out the window to the sprawl of sky visible beyond the rooftops. Maybe this was some sort of heavenly intervention. A dark bank of clouds was hunkering in the distance. Hmm.

The day was morphing into something entirely unexpected. Did she wish she'd tamed her hair into something more sophisticated, washed her face, put on something other than her reliable skirt and navy wrap-over?

Yes.

Did she resent her former dance captain for needling her into coming out of her cozy fortress of a flat for a job she didn't want?

Yes.

Coming along had seemed to be the only way to get everyone off her back. Now that she had, she wasn't entirely sure she wanted to leave without learning a bit more about Cole Manning. And the puppy. It was cute. Mishmash mutt cute. One ear up, one ear down. Forlorn expression on its face. A little bit like looking in the mirror.

She narrowed her eyes at Cole. He was cute, too. But his ears matched. *Hmm*.

Nah. Nope. She wasn't going to do it. Now wasn't the time to open up. She hadn't even come close to sorting things out for herself and she'd vowed not to let anyone in—let alone renowned Dr. Fancy Dance Clinic Manning—until she could face the world, aka her family, with pride.

Her fingers stilled as her gaze slipped away from Dr. Charming's expectant gaze. She had been wrong to come. She wasn't ready. Not yet.

"I'm sorry," she mumbled, pressing herself up and out of the chair. "Maybe another time."

"Ah, but that's where you're wrong." Cole leaned back in his chair, hands lacing behind his head. "This is a limited-time-only offer."

She pressed a hand against the wall to stabilize herself as a hit of dizziness unbalanced her.

The sensation was growing familiar. Food shopping hadn't exactly been topping her list of things to do. Very little topped her list of things to do these days. What was the point when her entire life's ambition—not to mention her daily routine for the past twelve years—had disappeared at the end of a poorly executed *plié*?

A *plié*! Of all the ways to shatter your dreams into smithereens…

"So what's on offer, Dancing Doctor? Is this a job with benefits?" The words were out before she could stem them. *Oops.* She doubted they were printed on his business card. Not that he'd shown her one.

"I doubt anyone who has seen me dance would call me that."

Maybe not. But he didn't seem to mind.

His full lips opened into a broad smile. There was a little gap between his front teeth that was… Ooh, *mój boże…* It was sexy! Lina hadn't felt anything close to even a hint of desire for months—okay fine, longer—and now twice in the space of an hour? Her giddy nerve endings were fighting her very best poker face for supremacy.

What was he doing being all good-looking and thirty-something anyway? She'd thought Dr. Cole Manning would look more—more academic, have furrows in his brow and maybe some white hair. A big shock of it. Who had put that dimple on his cheek when he smiled? That thing was about as close to irresistible as it got. *And on top of that a puppy?* Life was testing her. Hard.

Lina stopped herself from chewing on her lip. And ogling. It could come across as flirtatious. She didn't do relationships. Not now—and she certainly didn't do flirting. Particularly at job interviews.

"I hope you're not trying to find another project—another success story. No headlines to be made here, I'm afraid."

Did his jaw just twitch? Hard to tell. Maybe she'd hit a sore point. Well, too bad. This time of day was normally when she took a first-class nap. Then again, she'd been taking a few too many of those lately.

"Why's that? What's so bad about your story?" he challenged.

Uh. Apart from the totally obvious fact that she'd never dance again? She held her cane out between them. "It's a bit too late for a full recovery."

He let the words hang between them for a moment. She liked that he didn't offer her the over-sympathetic expressions she'd had from all of the hospital staff when she'd been in recovery. The piteous looks had made her blood boil. She wasn't someone to be pitied. She was someone who…

Who…

Well, that was as yet to be decided, wasn't it?

Lina shifted her position as the wind dropped out of her sails. She didn't exactly know who she was these days. All she knew for sure was what she wasn't—a ballerina.

"I don't think I'd be much good at delivering messages quickly for you."

"Lina, I'm pleased to inform you En Pointe is part of the modern era. We receive and deliver our messages by telephone—not foot messenger these days." And there came that slow smile again—like the sun coming out from beneath a cloud. Warming, wrapping round her like a protective blanket.

She considered him skeptically. Why was he doing this? Interviewing *her*—the least likely candidate for the job?

"And we have the latest in ergonomic chairs ready and waiting to be whirled in." He gave her a playful smile and showed off his chair's three-sixty spin. "If whirling in wheelie chairs between taking calls is your thing."

She lifted an eyebrow and gave him a "yeah, right" look.

"And, of course, a whole lot of other things you are familiar with." Cole's face turned serious as he began to rattle off the seemingly endless list of injuries a ballet dancer—any dancer—could come across on any given day, at any given moment. Just. Like. Her.

He rose and crossed to a table where coffee and tea supplies were in abundance. Was that how he fueled himself?

"You're Polish, right? So I presume you take coffee?"

She nodded.

"How do you take it?"

"White—no, black." Her eyes caught his as she heard herself say, "I like both."

She wasn't talking about coffee anymore.

Heat instantly began to sear Lina's cheeks and she forced herself to look away. Anywhere but at Cole. He was obviously mixed race and—*słodkie niebiosa*—he'd turned out perfectly. Not that she was attracted to him or anything. She was more used to being surrounded by gorgeous men at work than not. It had just…been a while.

She watched as he flicked the switch on the kettle before he opened a packet—definitely from a specialty shop—and poured a healthy pile of grounds directly into a waiting *cafetière*, grinned and gave her a wink. Measuring didn't seem to be his thing.

"I hope you like it strong."

Her tummy fluttered.

Er…what was *that*? She didn't have tummy flutters. She had—well, she wasn't quite sure what she had but she wasn't a schoolgirl with strings of pastel-colored butterflies dancing gaily around her insides. She was a woman on the verge of figuring out what to do with the whole rest of her entire life now that all her hopes and dreams had careened straight over the horizon.

"So, tell me more about this job. Nine to five and see you later, boss man?"

"Something like that. Here, have some biscuits." Cole tossed her the packet. Guess formality wasn't his thing, either. Refreshing after years of ballet where every breath she'd taken, every gesture she'd made, *everything* had been based on exacting tradition.

Cole settled himself back into his chair after

handing her a mug of coffee. "It's pretty straight-forward. Answering the phones, checking clients in…" He pointedly looked at his coffee. "Making sure the milkman has come."

"You have a milkman?" The information brought an unchecked smile to her lips. She'd grown up in a small village where the milkman, the baker and butcher had still been everyday sights. Everyday *jobs*.

"Sure do." Cole grinned back. "Why? Were you a milkmaid in your past?"

"No." The smile abruptly tightened into a gri-mace. Her best friend from school had followed in her mother's footsteps and milked her father's dairy herd. They made cheese and, on special oc-casions, ice cream—but mostly it was delicious, creamy milk and very, very hard work which, by all accounts, she still did.

Lina had led a different life. Her parents had scrimped and saved and sacrificed so that their daughter could pursue her dream of becoming a ballerina.

Which one of them was happier now? she won-dered.

She saw Cole watching her intently. Best to keep

on track. Trips down memory lane weren't of any use now. "The job?"

"Right. The job." Cole had to stop himself from physically shaking his head to put himself back in the moment. He'd been outright staring and was pretty sure Lina had caught him at it. He doubted he'd disguised it as an interested-physician look. It had been a bald and outright I-wish-I-knew-more-about-you look. He cleared his throat.

"As I said, it's pretty straightforward. It doesn't pay a high salary, but if you're happy to have a trial run—a week to start with to see if you're interested and then three months before we sign a full contract—we open at nine a.m. I'd expect you at eight." He named a figure and noticed Lina's eyes widen ever so slightly. It wouldn't put her in designer heels but it would pay her rent. The last time he'd checked, box-office staff at the City of London Ballet were receiving more an hour than members of the corps de ballet. Everyone needed to make a living, and fallen prima ballerinas were no different.

"So?"

Lina still hadn't said anything. She took a sip of her coffee, her face unreadable.

"And if after one day I decide this isn't for me?"

"We hire someone else. Simple as…"

"Simple as what?"

Cole laughed. "I don't know. I heard someone cool on television say it and thought I'd have a go. Clearly, I'm not down with the hipsters."

Lina took a bite of biscuit, hand curled protectively in front of her mouth as she chewed, rather than risk a reply. He didn't need to be in with any crowd. Cole Manning was in a class of his own. She closed her eyes as the sugary sweetness of the biscuit melted into nothing on her tongue. It tasted like home. The one place she couldn't go until she could show her parents she'd been worth the effort.

She looked at Cole again. He seemed genuine enough. As did the job offer.

A receptionist job. Well… She tried to keep her dejected sigh silent. At least she knew she was physically up to it. Talking to people—talking to *dancers*—all day might not come so easily.

She looked away from him, teasing at a pile of invisible flower petals on the floor. She didn't want him to see how much she needed the job. Her foot automatically shaped itself into an elegant turnout as it swiped the "petals" to the side of the room with a controlled semicircle of movement. That much she could do.

"Cole!" A woman appeared at the doorway and gave the frame a quick double knock. "We need you in Reception right away."

It was then that Lina tuned into the noises outside Cole's office. There was the sound of a young woman crying. Periodically broken by an occasional heated wail. She knew that feeling. She knew it down to her bones.

"All right, Lina? Are we good?" Cole rose quickly to his feet, moving the puppy's basket to the floor.

"So I already have the job?" She couldn't help but let some cynicism sneak into her voice. This whole thing was sounding more and more like some sort of setup.

"Let me check what's happening out there and then see how we go, shall we?"

CHAPTER TWO

"IT HURTS!" THE teenager's face was a picture of pure unadulterated agony. She was on the floor, knees slightly bent, back hunched over, and a wash of tears wetting her cheeks.

"It looks like it hurts," Cole agreed. He was never one of these doctors who brushed away the pain. If it hurt it hurt. Plain as. Apart from which the poor girl's foot was already thick with heat and swelling. If he had to guess? A serious sprain—level two. A possible tear in the ATFL? Nothing life-altering, but it would certainly keep her out of pointe shoes for a couple of months, and for a young girl like this—thirteen or fourteen—it would feel like a lifetime. He looked up at the mother, who also had tears in her eyes. He raised his eyebrows in lieu of asking what had happened.

"I dropped her before we reached the sofa."

"You mean you carried her in here?" Cole was impressed. It was a bit of a hike from the pavement.

"We were just about there and…" Her hand flew to her mouth in horror.

"You did well. No additional harm done. Just a bit of ego bruising, from the looks of things." He nodded to the mother before quickly returning his attention to her daughter. "You're all right, darlin', aren't you?" The teen gave an unconvinced nod before Cole looked back at her mother. "Shall we get her up and into an exam room?"

"Please. I am so— The day's just been…I tried…"

Cole rose, put a hand on the woman's shoulder and gave her a reassuring smile. Parents were often more traumatized than their child. From the looks of the number pinned on her daughter's chest she'd been at the London Ballet Grand Prix. The biggest day on a young ballerina's calendar. There would be no scholarships or job offers for her this year.

"Let me help. Can I have your arm?"

Cole looked down at the sound of Lina's softly accented voice. She was totally focused on the girl.

"What piece were you doing?" Lina instinctively sought to distract the girl from her injury.

Cole moved round to help Lina raise the girl from the ground but watched curiously to see how she dealt with a traumatized dancer. They shared common ground. It could be useful.

"I was doing the 'Spring Concerto.'" The girl only just held back a sob.

"Vivaldi?" Lina's face lit up. "What a wonderful choice. And your contemporary piece?" She sat back on her heels and looked at the girl seriously. "You *did* have a contemporary piece, right?"

"It was 'Spiegel im Spiegel.'"

"Are you kidding? That's one of my favorites. I used to dance to that one a lot."

"Used to?" The girl swiped away some of her tears, missing Lina's microscopic wince.

"What's your name?" Lina asked.

"Vonnie."

"Beautiful." She tucked an arm around the girl's small waist and began to raise her into a wheelchair she must have brought in. Resourceful. Cole found himself beginning to rethink the "just a favor" part of his agreement. Maybe she would be a good hire.

"I'm Lina. Shall we get you to X-ray?"

It was all Cole could do not to laugh. Lina didn't

have the slightest clue where X-ray was and how she'd magicked a wheelchair out of nowhere was impressive...a picture of confidence. And, more importantly, she'd engaged Vonnie enough to begin to stem the flow of tears. Impressive for someone who hadn't seemed keen to spend her day with working dancers.

"Actually, can you put any weight on it?" Cole was the doctor here. Probably wise to take charge of this scenario.

Vonnie wrapped an arm round Lina's shoulder and, with Cole's help, heaved herself up.

"Have you already put ice on it? Kept it elevated on the ride over here?"

"Yes," Vonnie snuffled. "As soon as it ha-ha-happened!"

Uh-oh. Those tears were back again.

"Lina, I'll take Vonnie to X-ray, all right?"

The young girl twisted round, her face wreathed in anxiety, one of Lina's hands clutched in her own. "No! Please don't make her go. She *understands* me."

Lina looked over at Cole and gave him the Polish version of a Gallic shrug.

"Fine. But you'll have to leave the room during

the X-ray." Cole stepped away from the handles of the wheelchair and handed over steering duty to Lina. She wanted to work here? She could prove it. "I'll lead the way, shall I?"

Cole tipped his head from side to side as he took in the extent of the injury. Swelling could hide things, but X-rays didn't lie. He'd been right. It was a typical grade-two ballerina sprain—a tear of the anterior talofibular ligament with lateral swelling.

"So what do you say? Eight weeks until she dances again?"

"Mmm…something like that."

In the tiny dark room, with only the X-ray board spreading a low-grade wash of light, having Lina so close, Cole had to rethink how wise a move it would be to hire her. He was attracted to her. And not just your average gee-you're-good-looking sort of attraction. He was fighting a Class-A desire to spin her round, pull her into his arms and find out how she tasted, how she would respond to his touch. None of which would really be appropriate in a professional environment.

"It'll be hard for her to hear…on top of missing out at the Grand Prix."

"Believe me, I've delivered my share of bad news."

Lina noticed Cole's change of tone instantly. Almost felt it, they were so close. There was something deep-seated in his words. Grief? Rage? She couldn't quite tell which, but maybe the rumors about him fighting demons was true. Not such a lighthearted Southern gent after all.

"I'd better get out of your way so you can let her know."

"Yes, that'd be great." Cole batted away the words, "I mean, I need to do this with the patient… Protocol," he added, as if it were necessary. She knew the drill. She wasn't a doctor so why should she have access to Vonnie's appointment? It was for her mother to be there for her, and from the sound of approaching voices she would shortly be with her.

"Okay, well…it was nice to meet you. I guess I'll wait to hear from you?"

She turned to give him a goodbye grin and got as far as turning. Right down to her very toes she felt the impact of the aquamarine of his eyes. A shame it would be the last time she was going to see them. A shame about a lot of things.

"How long has it been?" Cole's voice broke into the quiet, indicating she should follow him to his office.

"Since what?"

"Since you've had a proper meal?"

Lina stiffened.

A while.

But not because of— *Oof. Honestly?* She balled up her jacket and protectively clutched it to her tummy. As if that would stop the jig-jag of emotions bouncing around in there. She liked eating as much as the next person. She just hadn't been able to get it together and money was tight. Supertight. Things she most certainly wasn't going to admit to Mr. Doesn't-Like-to-Poke-His-Nose-Into-Other-People's-Business. Ha! That'd be about right.

"I'm fine."

"I didn't say otherwise." The puppy whined. Cole pulled the wicker basket up from the floor to have a peek and give the pooch's muzzle a little rub. Not that he was growing fond of the thing.

"Look." He gave Lina a pointed look. "This guy

needs some grub and so do I. Why don't you join us for dinner? My treat."

"No, thank you. I'm not hungry."

Lina's tummy rumbled. Loudly.

Cole grabbed a couple of charts and a prescription pad from his desk before squaring himself to her. "After I finish with Vonnie, join me. Us. I know a little place down the road. Go have a nosy around Reception while you're waiting. See what you think. Consider it part two of your interview. You don't have the job yet."

Er… "Okay." Lina said the word to his back as he headed out of the office but got a thumbs-up as he disappeared round the corner. Hmm…

The puppy whimpered again and Lina found herself gently extracting him from his willow basket nest.

Poor little thing had a splint on his tiny back leg and looked terrifically sorry for himself. She gave an appreciative snort. "We all have our moments. Don't we, Puppy?" Now, to see what the future had in store…

A good nosy around and Lina felt none the wiser. Actually, it hadn't been much of a snoop session.

She'd just gone into the reception area, plopped herself and Puppy down on one of the—very nice—sofas and thumbed through a magazine or two. Sitting behind the reception desk would have seemed too much like interest. It would have been akin to acknowledging how much she really needed the job. So reading magazines and enjoying the serene atmosphere, now that most of the practitioners had gone for the day, was what she did, happily enjoying the latest celebrity gossip and fashion mags… And then she hit *Dance Monthly.*

The cover story nearly sent her running for the hills: "Down and Out: Are the Fallen Forgotten?"

Against her will, tears sprang to her eyes. They may as well have put her face on the cover. Talk about cruel! She fought the growing tickle in her throat and nose, tightened her eyes, scrunched her forehead as much as she could, willing the pain to go away. Would there ever come a day when things wouldn't hurt this much? It was hard to believe. Impossible even.

"Dr. Manning said you were still here!" A tearstained but smiling Vonnie appeared in Reception with a pair of crutches and her leg done up in a pneumatic walker. Lina jumped to her feet and shook away the remains of her own tears. She didn't know why, but having helped Vonnie, for even a few moments earlier, had given her a boost. It would hardly do for the teen to find her blubbing on her own.

"Remember not to put any weight on that for three weeks!"

Cole appeared beside Vonnie with a bag of what she assumed to be treatment aids. Cooling gels, compression wraps, anti-inflammatories. She knew the drill.

"I know." Vonnie sighed melodramatically, and rolled her eyes in Lina's direction before singsonging, "RICE, RICE, RICE, RICE, RICE!"

"That's right, young lady," Cole replied in a stentorian tone Lina hadn't heard from him before. "And what does it stand for?"

"OMG, I practically came out of the womb knowing what that stood for!"

Cole crossed his arms and gave her a very good "I'm waiting" face. Lina could easily see him being a parent, willing to wait as long as it took for the child to clean their room, finish their homework, whatever… She wondered what— No, she didn't. She didn't wonder that at all!

"Rest, ice, compression and elevation. Are you happy?" Vonnie's tone was more teasing than truculent so whatever they'd discussed in the exam room had put her in a better mood. Her mother emerged with coats and handbags and a couple of tutus Lina hadn't noticed before.

"Ooh, look at these—they are wonderful!" Lina couldn't help herself.

"Do you really think so?" Vonnie's mum flushed with pleasure as Lina nodded emphatically. "I made them."

"They're amazing." Lina meant it. From the very bottom of her heart. Her own mother, to save money on the countless tutus she'd required, had stitched and stitched and stitched for her, as well. "You've got a wonderful mother, Vonnie." Lina gave the girl's shoulder a squeeze. "You make sure you let her know how much you appreciate her."

"I will!" Vonnie replied, working her way across Reception and out the door. She might, mused Lina. Or she might not. Lina hoped she had done the latter, but was never sure it had been enough.

One day…she would let her mother know just how heartfelt her gratitude was. One day.

"So, I guess that's us! Just another day at En Pointe!" Cole shrugged on a wool blazer, scooped up the puppy in his basket from the sofa and gestured with his head toward the front door with a smile. "Are you ready?"

Cole took about three seconds to examine the menu before offering the waitress a smile and his order.

"I'll have the spaghetti carbonara, a fresh salad, some garlic bread and—uh—Rover, here, will have a bit of plain chicken and some rice. In a bowl. Is that doable?"

"Not a problem."

It was easy enough for Lina to see that anything Cole or "Rover" asked for wouldn't be a problem for the waitress, who had plonked herself down in the spare chair between the two of them. Lina may as well have been invisible for all the attention the waitress was paying her. Not that she minded. Going along to a job interview she'd been cajoled into was one thing, but being dragged out—okay, well, being *blackmailed* into going out to dinner was another.

"Who's the little puppy?" The server had on her best baby-talk voice now. "You're the little puppy! You're the little puppy!"

So much for the restaurant's no-dogs policy.

The waitress had already made a puppy-exception rule, and brought the little guy a bowl of water and a couple of itty-bitty raw carrots to gnaw on in case he was teething. Right now the pup's head was resting on the brim of the basket, lending him more supercute factor than anyone—or anything—should be allowed.

Cute factor or no, Lina was there for the sole purpose of securing the job. That was it.

"Lina?" Cole tipped his head in the waitress's direction. It was her turn to order. She'd scanned the prices and hadn't even bothered to look at the menu choices. One entrée was the equivalent of her weekly food budget.

"Don't worry." Cole reached across and covered her hand in his. "I'll take it out of your first paycheck."

Lina tugged her hand away and clenched it in her lap. She wasn't comfortable accepting help...

but it had been ages since she'd had a well-made restaurant meal. Gone were the days of being feted by London's social elite.

"The gnocchi, please. And a rocket salad." They were the least expensive items, but with the added bonus of reminding her of *pierogi*. *Pierogi!* Her mouth watered at the thought of her mother's *pierogi*. One day…she'd go home one day. Lina pursed her lips and handed the waitress her menu, who gave her a cursory glance, scribbled something on her notepad, then whirled off with a smile expressly for Cole's benefit.

Lina focused her attention on the puppy. Neutral territory. That's what she needed. Cole's hand on hers had been too close to feeling something— wanting something. She hadn't realized how curative the simple touch of a hand could be.

"He doesn't look like a Rover."

"No?" Cole rubbed a finger along the little guy's head. "What does he look like?"

As if by design, they both crossed their arms, leaned back and considered the puppy. He had a white muzzle that broadened into a wide stripe that led up to his forehead. Black took over from there. He had little brown arches over each eye, white paws and appeared slightly affronted at this very obvious inspection.

"Vladimir," Lina pronounced.

"Horace," Cole countered.

Lina shook her head. "No. He is not a Horace."

"How do you know he's not a Horace?"

"I just know." Lina gave Cole her best I-just-know look, then tipped her head to the left as if it would give her a different perspective. The puppy opened his eyes wider as if in anticipation of her coming out with the right name.

"Wojciech."

"I can't even pronounce that." Cole laughed. "How about Spot?"

"No!" Lina protested. "That's lazy. And look. Where do you see spots on this guy?" She lifted him up out of the basket. His back leg was in a little splint. She wanted to ask what had happened but felt herself already getting too involved with the puppy and with Cole. They both looked at her as if she held all the answers to the question at hand.

Despite herself, she couldn't help giving the puppy a little cuddle. It was impossible not to. She held him up again so that they were face-to-face. "What's your name, huh? *Jak masz na imię?*" The puppy scrunched his face into a mess of wrinkles before yawning widely in her face. Then he sneezed. Twice.

"Maybe he doesn't speak Polish."

"Maybe he doesn't speak American." She kept her gaze on the puppy.

Cole rearranged the cutlery at his place setting with a grin. "Go on, then, Polish puppy-whisperer. What's his name?"

Lina looked across at Cole once she had given the puppy a good long stare. "Igor."

"Igor," Cole repeated, as if he hadn't heard her correctly.

"Yes. Igor."

For the second time that day Lina's mood lifted as that smile of his peeled apart his lips and heated her insides as if he'd unleashed a swathe of warm sunlight.

"I like it. Looks like we've got ourselves a puppy name."

Lina handed Igor across to him, careful not to get his injured leg caught on anything. "No. *You* have yourself a puppy name. *And* a puppy."

Cole cradled the dog in the crook of his arm,

careful to adjust the little splinted leg so it could lie along his forearm. "Didn't I tell you? Part of the new job is dog walking. Once his leg heals, of course. Only until I find him a new home, of course."

"Yes, of course," Lina replied dubiously. Then the cogs started to whirl in a direction she didn't like. She could feel the smile on her lips press into a thin line. Part of her physio was to take regular walks. Longer and longer. She should be doing at least two or three kilometers a day by now. Cole would know that. And, having watched her walk to the restaurant, he would probably have assessed that she hadn't been taking as many walks as she had been advised to. She'd done countless laps of her flat but going out there—out *here*—where everyone could see her, judge her...she just hadn't been up to it. Igor pricked up his ears and gave her an expectant look. Her eyes shifted to Cole's face and he looked virtually the same—minus the furry muzzle. She couldn't help but laugh.

"Does anyone ever say no to you, Dr. Manning?"

The smile disappeared entirely from his eyes. "Oh, you'd be surprised."

* * *

When Lina excused herself to go to the ladies' room, Cole waited for the waitress to take away their empty plates and give a farewell coo to Igor before pulling his coat on. He was pretty sure he knew the server's life story by now but could honestly say he would leave the restaurant being none the wiser about the private life of Lina Keminsky. Not that prying had been his intention. They'd stuck to neutral topics when their food had arrived. And as much as Cole knew about how Reception worked, which, as it had turned out, wasn't all that much. He'd taken over the practice about a year ago from an old medical school friend who had run off to get married—a recurring theme at En Pointe—and things had been running like a well-oiled ship up until now. Not that the past hour with Lina hadn't lent a certain softening round the edges to the day.

It was pretty easy to tell she didn't like to talk about herself and she'd quickly sussed out the same was true for him—or perhaps she simply wasn't interested, which made a nice change. At home, or at least back in the United States, in the town where he'd grown up everyone knew everything about him. Back home everyone knew he'd had a fiancée—*had* being the crucial word. At twenty-six she'd been too young to die. Far too young. And her family was never going to let him forget it. So the fact that people generally kept themselves to themselves in London suited him to a T.

If what had happened to Lina had happened back home in North Carolina? There would've been a line of people at the door to her apartment, hands filled with bowls of potato salad, a platter of Grandma's best fried chicken, a warm, tea-towel-wrapped plate filled with buttery collard greens, someone's Great-Auntie Kay's to-die-for double-decker chocolate cake with the cherry filling people talked about so much at the church socials, and so on and so on until before you knew it the whole thing would turn into an Item of Interest in the "What's the Buzz" column of Maple Cove's local gazette. There was no escaping the caring embrace of a community like that one. Especially when your African-American father and Irish mother were pillars of the community. The local judge and the most sought-after doula? There was no surprise when the couple's son became a doctor engaged to the town's most promising lawyer! A smile twitched on his lips, then tightened.

He wasn't part of that community anymore.

He felt his teeth dig into his lower lip. It wasn't worth it. Opening that particular can of worms. His parents were good folk. They were just ambitious. For themselves and for him. So what if they hadn't been a huggy-kissy family? He'd made it, hadn't he? Decorum, status, success. They were paramount in the Manning household. And now that he was a doctor running one of Britain's most elite specialist clinics?

Nothing. None of it mattered.

The straight As at school, the letterman's jacket weighed down with athletic achievements, the Ivy League education, the long-awaited proposal… none of the graft he'd put in to win an approving smile or a hug had meant a bean after the accident. His parents had made that more than clear.

The flash of grief tugged his mouth downward.

So, no. He didn't like howdy-do-and-what-about-you? chitchat. Big-city anonymity had been suiting him just fine up to now.

But when it came to Lina? There was something

telling him she might be worth breaking unwritten rules for.

She'd deftly managed to unearth his dry sense of humor and, as it had turned out, she had Eastern European drollness down to a T. Her impersonation of the waitress going all googly-eyed over the puppy had had him in stitches. Not that he hadn't tried to hide it from her. He was going to be her boss after all and there were boundaries. Not that he'd managed to wrangle a "yes" out of her. If she did take the job, he'd have to remember that would be the extent of their relationship. A working one. He didn't do personal. And he definitely didn't do personal at work.

So why on earth had he invited her out to dinner? Not to mention let her name his puppy! Correction—*the* puppy. The puppy he was going to find a home for as soon as humanly possible.

He gave his head a scrub and snorted at the results. He'd given himself a grade-two once-over with his electric shaver that morning and wasn't so sure even could be an accurate description. Yet another thing to add to the list of things that had turned his day into a catalog of disasters. Maybe he'd just wanted a bit of company for dinner. Someone who plainly didn't want anything from him. No answers, no advice, no decisions. That suited him perfectly. If he could just shake off his attraction to her, he could go back to being cool, calm and collected Cole. The one who left his emotions at home. His parents, he thought with a bitter twist, would've been proud. At last! He was now just like them.

"You look like a snake bit you in the face."

"Thanks and you look—" Cole stopped himself. He'd been about to say beautiful. "You look ready for a break from Igor and me."

Cole automatically reached for her coat and helped her slip into it. His mother had drilled that into him. "Manners don't make a man sexist, they make a man polite, and no one ever had a quibble about 'polite.'"

"You're too kind."

If only she knew. Cruel to be kind was more like it.

As Lina slipped her arms into the sleeves and shrugged the coat over her shoulders, Cole was struck by how fragile her neck looked. Before they'd gone out she'd swept her hair up into some sort of semitamed twist, and a few tendrils had come loose and were brushing along the length of her neck, her shoulders. It was taking some serious control to stop himself from reaching forward and letting the pad of his thumb or the length of his finger draw down the length of her neck. He could just as easily imagine fastening a set of pearls round her neck, then dipping his lips to kiss the bare, pale swoop of skin between her neck and shoulder—

Lina turned around abruptly, and their noses nearly collided. Cole instinctively grabbed hold of her so she could steady herself but in that moment—and it was just a moment—with her face within kissing distance, her eyes caught with his, Cole knew he'd have to channel his deepest powers of control to ensure he only saw Lina for what she was—a potential candidate for the reception job. A job she hadn't even committed to accepting. Hey! Maybe she wouldn't take it. It'd probably be for the best.

She blinked. He hadn't noticed the light color of her lashes before. He'd been too busy exploring the soft green hue of her— *Hold your fire, there, soldier!* No one's going down that road just yet. Or at all.

"Right. I'd better get Igor back to get some snuggly time. Or something like that." He regrouped and made his voice more doctorly. "Sleep. Puppies need sleep. Lots of it." Cole took a broad step away from Lina and scooped up the basket where—up until that very moment—Igor had actually been sleeping quite contentedly. The puppy quirked a sleepy eyebrow at him. Lina shot him a similar look for good measure. Fine. He felt like an idiot. *Could we all just get a move on now?*

"Okay. I'll see you at eight o'clock tomorrow morning, then?" She shifted her feet nervously.

Cole didn't bat an eyelid.

So, she *was* taking the job. Bang went that solution.

Maybe she'd hate it and this little frisson— or whatever it was that was going on between them—would be short-lived.

"Yes. Perfect. See you then."

Lina bent to give Igor a little scratch on the head. *"Dobranoc kochanie, Igor. Tu jest nic!"*

"What's that?"

Sweet nothings for the pooch? Or something about their near miss in the kissing department? He scrubbed his hand along his chin. *Terrific.*

Now paranoia had set in. His former reception-ist had better be having one hell of an elopement!

"Nothing." She tightened her coat round her slim frame and gave him a cursory farewell wave. "See you in the morning."

"You bet. With bells on!"

She didn't turn around. Which was for the best.

With bells on?

This wasn't going to just be a trial period. It was going to be a trial by fire. And Cole knew he'd be the one racing across the burning coals.

It was cold enough in the flat that Lina wasn't going to risk taking her hand out from underneath the downy duvet to give herself a good old conk on the head. What had she been thinking? Accepting the job at En Pointe? Pure unadulterated crazy.

She'd heard Cole worked miracles with his patients—but getting her to break her months-long hibernation? He hadn't pushed her, but there was definitely a won't-take-no aura about him. If she believed in that sort of thing. From what she'd gathered—and it wasn't that much—he was more of a take-it-or-leave-it type. He'd seen and done a lot in his lifetime. It was impressive. And he hadn't got where he was from sitting in his flat, moping. The train he was driving? It was ready to leave the station. If you wanted to be on the Manning Express, jump on fast!

So she'd jumped.

It was a matter of necessity after all. But that didn't stop her stomach from churning. Or the odd butterfly from taking a teasing swoop and whoosh around her tummy.

The tick-tick of the clock suddenly seemed louder than Big Ben's bongs.

In a matter of hours she was going from seeing no one but the postman—or his hand, at least— to answering the phone and sitting on Reception at Britain's finest dance injury clinic.

She chanced sticking a finger out of the duvet to give her cold nose a scratch. Once she got her first paycheck she could get the heat turned back on. Oh, to be warm! She scrunched her eyes tightly against the streetlight conveniently beaming directly into her bedroom and let herself—just for a moment—picture summertime in her childhood village. There might not have been much money coming into the homes there but it was undoubtedly a rural idyll. Vast wildflower meadows sprawling up into the foothills of the mountains. Snow-capped peaks diminishing with the heat of the summer sun. A broad river teeming with shoals of fish and a seemingly endless array of birds. Maybe when his leg healed, she, Cole and Igor could find a park somewhere…

Maybe she, Cole and Igor *nothing.*

It was work. A job. They were not a magic trio. Cole was her boss. Igor was a—a patient? And she was going to answer the telephone. That was it. Working at En Pointe was a way to pay the rent and dig herself out of this ridiculous hole of unpaid bills she'd gotten herself into. Then, *maybe,* she could think about what to do next. There was no point in getting attached to anything because one thing life had taught her for certain was that nothing lasted forever.

But even as the thought crossed her mind, Lina couldn't help a smile from tugging at her lips— or stop the small burst of pride she felt for having said yes to the job. It was a baby step. But it was a step. Her smile broadened as an image of Cole leaning against his office desk flitted across her mind's eye. He looked all casual, relaxed and in control at the same time. Someone who was comfortable in his skin. Maybe he was a miracle worker. For the first time in a long time, apart from feeling scared out of her wits, she felt—just a teensy tiny bit—as if she just might be looking forward to a brand-new day.

CHAPTER THREE

"YOU DON'T REALLY know what you're talking about, do you?"

"Don't be ridiculous. Of course, I…" Cole tried to look affronted and then realized it was pointless. Apart from the fact that Lina's office look was about as pencil-skirt-tastic as a woman could get, he didn't have a clue how the phone system worked.

"Sorry, Lina. I'm newfangled. Just give me one of these…" he pulled the latest model mobile phone from his pocket "…and I'm fine. One of these?" He eyed the multiline reception system like it had just flown in from outer space and waved his hand dismissively at it. "All Greek. Or should I say Polish?" He gave her a wink chased up by a meaningful look. It was meant to convey confidence. Or a boss-like jocularity. Lina frowned in response.

"Dr. Manning, you're paying me to answer the

phone—so I will answer the phone. Now, step aside, please, and go do your doctor thing." Lina sat down decisively in her very nice chair and shooed him out from behind the reception area. This was her turf now. Not to mention the fact it was a bit too cozy having the two of them behind the desk. Very cozy. He'd been there long enough for her to divine that Cole's mysterious, exotic man scent was not the coffee, the dog or anything else—it was *eau de Cole*. Olfactory heaven. And strictly off the menu! She might have to mouth-breathe in future to resist the urge to bury her face in his chest and just inhale. And resist she would.

This was a chance for her to get a grip on her life—not play googly-eyes with the scrumptious doctor. She shot him her best "scoot" look, more for herself than for him—but it worked. Which was satisfying.

"Don't blame me for being all addlepated this morning. It's entirely Igor's fault. He kept me up most of the night with his crying."

"You didn't stick him in one of those horrible cages, did you?" Lina blurted. She couldn't help it. She had a soft spot for Igor. And Cole.

No. Just Igor. Not Cole. He was an ogre. Well, not an ogre exactly…

He raised up his hands with an irascible twist to his lips. "Guilty as charged." Then his expression softened. "That is, until about twenty minutes later when I couldn't stand it anymore and brought him into my room. He stole my pillow."

Lina couldn't help but smile at the picture Cole painted. So he was a softie at heart. A bit different from the pull-your-own-socks-up portrait he'd painted of himself last night.

Cole abruptly pulled out a thick stack of colored sticky notes from his pocket and plonked them on her desk before hightailing it to his office. He'd already given Lina enough office supplies to last a month. She hardly needed more! Not to mention the tour of the clinic, each and every one of the therapy rooms, the changings rooms—separate for staff and patients—the sauna, the steam room, the water-therapy center and the staff kitchen—complete with a tour of the contents of the fridge-freezer. "Best to put your names on things if you really want to eat them." Talk about a worrywart!

She eyed the phone system warily. Then again…

Okay. Release the breath you've been holding

for the past twenty minutes. Three. Two. One. Fresh breath in... She watched as Cole turned the corner into his office, where he'd already stashed Igor in his basket... *And now you're on your own.*

The telltale tremble began in her hands. She shook them. Hard. It always worked before she went onstage, so why not here?

So what if telling Cole she knew how it all worked had been bravura? At least it had been effective enough to get him out of her hair. Her well-groomed and twisted-into-a-French-knot hair, thank you very much indeed. Sleeping hadn't really worked out so well the previous night, so a bit of overdue grooming had taken up the dawn hours. Not to mention the fact she was wearing her Sunday—and Monday through Saturday—best. She had one office-appropriate outfit and until she got a bit of money in the bank it would have to do. Not that she was planning on doing this forever. Not by a long shot. She was just playing a role—Tragic Receptionist. She'd even worn her old reading glasses from school for good measure.

Truthfully? Lina needed all the exterior armor she could get her hands on if she was going to convince herself, let alone everyone she would have to come into contact with, that she could do this job. And do it well. Turned out there was a lot more to it than picking up the phone and saying hello.

Answering the phones, greeting patients, pulling up medical records, making appointments, ordering flowers, milk, fruit, office supplies, updating staff schedules—*erp!*

She forced herself to take another deep breath in lieu of short-circuiting. Cole had left a lot of details out when he'd offered her the position. The only thing she'd really cared about had been the paycheck. Served her right. It was all she could do not to run out the door and go back to her bed and curl up in a protective little ball. It was too much all at once. If she tried to remember every single bit of information she'd have to learn in the next five minutes, her mind could just…very possibly…explode. Not to mention the torture of having to smile and offer warm greetings to working ballerinas all day long. The clinic, it seemed, mostly worked with dancers who could make a full recovery. It explained why her dance company hadn't really pushed for the clinic to take her on as a patient. Not that she would've been able to foot what she imagined would be a very large bill.

The air whooshed across her lips in a panicky sigh. She sucked in a fresh breath of air and forced herself to think of the plus side of her conundrum. She needed to regain the control she knew she could impose on herself.

Once she had a bit of money in the bank she would be able to move on. Who knew what might be out there, waiting for her, apart from a big black void of nothingness? There might be rainbows and daffodils…and unicorns and horses that flew with wax wings that melted at the first sign of spring.

Okay, Lina. Get a grip.

Right now there was no money in the bank and nowhere to move on to. So, that being the case, she was stuck here pretending she knew how to be a receptionist. A blinking light on the phone caught her eye. She glanced at the wall clock. Nine on the dot. She poised her finger over the button, popped on the headset, blew out another steadying breath and here went nothing!

Lina pressed the button and greeted the caller

as she'd been instructed, "En Pointe, this is Lina. May I help you?"

Silence.

She pressed the button again. "En Pointe, this is Lina. May I help you?"

Nothing.

Despite her best efforts, her mouth went dry. Just a little. Then another light started to blink. Panic started to set in. Another line lit up. The front door opened and a woman wearing bright purple scrubs entered and gave Lina a broad smile.

"Hi! Are you the new Scarlet?"

"Who?"

"Scarlet—the eloping receptionist," she explained, extending a hand across the high reception counter. "I'm Gemma Holland, one of the physios. Sports massage by day, aspiring osteopath by night."

Lina went to shake her hand but then thought she'd better try and answer the three calls coming in, and in swinging her hand back round she managed to get tangled in the headset wire and pull it free from the phone.

"Isn't it annoying?" Gemma smiled, unfazed as Lina's discombobulation grew. "I worked on the desk for a year and Cole still hasn't understood the importance of a wireless headset."

"You worked on Reception?" Lina couldn't hide her surprise.

"Yeah. A few of us have—before we qualified. Here…" She walked round the counter, plugged in the headset, popped it on, quickly and efficiently took the three calls and then turned to Lina with a mischievous expression. "Did Cole give you your 'training'?"

"If you call pointing at it and saying, 'That's the beast' as training."

"That's what I thought. Don't worry. I'll give you a quick run-through before my first patient arrives. Cole's useless. He doesn't do front of house."

Lina smiled at the term generally reserved for the theatre. She wondered if Gemma had been a dancer. She certainly had the figure for it. Had she been injured, too? There was a part of her that would love to have someone to confide in, make the world feel a bit less lonely.

Gemma quickly talked her through the system, which turned out not to be so complicated after all. "Just flick this switch here on the side and then punch the blinking light..." By the time Gemma had wished her luck and disappeared down the corridor, Lina felt a tiny bit more grounded.

Answering the phones? Check! She turned as the front door opened again. More staff and, from the look of the girl using crutches, the first patient of the day. Now all she needed to do was figure out how to do the four thousand other things the En Pointe receptionist was responsible for and everything would be fine.

Cole gave Igor a little scratch under the chin. It was five o'clock and about the ninety-thousandth time he'd checked his watch. He'd been itching to go out and check on Lina all day, but had thought she'd shy away from any sort of special treatment. He liked to be thrown in at the deep end and something told him—on that front—they were cut from the same cloth.

She'd need to find out on her own if she was cut out for the job. Not that he would've been much help anyhow. At least with the technical side of things. Yes, he could've introduced her to everyone—but a quick interoffice memo did the same thing, and more efficiently. So, yes, it was throwing Lina in at the deep end, but he wasn't in the business of coddling. So he'd done it surreptitiously. A handful of the therapists at EP had been in her shoes over the course of the years. Ballerinas, modern dancers, even circus performers who had, through either catastrophic injury or prescient decision-making, opted for a life in health care rather than completely destroy their bodies. Not everyone stayed. Not everyone left. He had to admit he hoped Lina would at least see through the week—and after that the three-month trial. At the very least, it would get her back out in the world and give her a bit of money in the bank. Not to mention buy her some time to think about her options, her future. As if it was any of his business and he cared at all. Which he did not.

Igor stretched out on his desk, paying little regard to the files Cole had been trying to read.

"Thanks for the respect, pal."

A light knock on Cole's door brought the puppy upright with a small yelp.

"Sorry, Igor. How's the little bitty poochpooch?" Gemma crooned, all eyes for the puppy and none for Cole, whose office she normally wouldn't have entered without an invitation. He obviously had some sort of invisible force field around him, screaming *Give me my space*, and it usually worked. Puppies apparently rendered it useless.

"Do you want him? Comes free with basket?" Cole asked, semihopefully.

"No way. He's cute, but I don't have the lifestyle for a dog." Gemma smiled. "Besides, my boss is a real whip-cracker. He wouldn't let me bring him to work."

Cole smirked. "Yeah. I hear he's a real hardass." They both considered Igor, now shifting Cole's paperwork about to make a more comfortable bed for himself.

"How do you think it happened?" Gemma pointed to the splint still weighing down Igor's leg.

"Scarlet said he'd been rescued from a violent home, along with five brothers and sisters."

"Ooh! He must be missing them, poor little thing. Are you sad to be all alone in the world?" Gemma gave Igor's ears little single-fingered sympathy strokes.

"Hmm." Cole couldn't help but think of his family and how much he missed them. Not to mention his fiancée. Deaths from car crashes had just been one in a sea of medical statistics until it had hit home. His home. His heart. He rubbed at his chin. A change of topic would be good about now.

"Hey—where'd you find Lina?"

Not that topic!

"Oh, her name cropped up when…"

"When?" Gemma not so helpfully prodded a finger, teasing the shorter ends of her freeform hairdo into little spikes.

Technically, the answer wasn't confidential, but he didn't think it would be appropriate to tell her about the telephone call from the head of the ballet. Then again, he'd been very clear to them he wasn't taking Lina on as a patient. Not that he'd actually planned on making her an employee. The whole thing was meant to have been a meaningless favor. What a mess!

He scribbled a couple of doodles on the side of his notebook to buy time. Feeling so protective about someone he hardly knew was a new experience. It was instinctive, not wanting the staff to know any more than Lina wanted them to know until she was good and ready to share. He knew firsthand that was one of the biggest steps forward in healing—a step he hadn't exactly taken in his own life.

"Her name came up when I was at the rehearsal hall the other day," he fibbed. "She seemed like she'd know her way round our specialist jargon."

"Wasn't she the one who shattered the ball in her hip joint?"

Cole sat up sharply. Lina obviously valued her privacy and he didn't want to "out" her before she'd had a chance to settle in, know that she was in safe territory.

"It was in the *Dance Monthly*," Gemma continued, oblivious to the internal battle Cole was having. "Apparently she out-*Giselle*d the best of them. Before the accident. I thought she looked familiar. It was a hard article to read. I hope she didn't see it."

Public figures equaled public domain. Just as it had been when the local rag had got hold of the news he had been the one to switch off his fiancée's life-support system. They hadn't cared about Katie's living will or the absolute, straight-through-to-the-marrow heartbreak it had taken to see her wishes through. All they'd said was that one of Maple Cove's brightest lights had been

ANNIE O'NEIL

switched off by her own fiancé. And with that one headline all of the trust his patients had had in him had evaporated like a thin mist.

"What can I do for you, Gemma? Apart from offering some puppy therapy?"

His colleague grinned at him, perched on the side of his desk and scooped up the dog for a proper cuddle. "You know the sports massage therapy course I've been giving over at the continuing education center?"

"Yes. That's been going well for you?"

"Brilliantly. But I've reached the point where my students need some guinea pigs."

"And?" Cole warily asked.

"And…I was wondering if I could use the staff here at the clinic one day after work. Like a treat! On a Tuesday or Wednesday evening perhaps? When you— I mean, no one has anything going on socially."

"Speak for yourself, Gemma."

The physio didn't even try to contain her laughter. "Since when did you start going out on the razzle, Manning?"

"That's Dr. Manning to you." Cole tried to put on his best stentorian tone, but he and Gemma were the same age so it was ridiculous to try and come across as her older, wiser boss. They'd just had different career paths. His had involved tunnel vision and hers had been more circuitous—including having a life outside work. Going with the flow.

He stemmed an ironic bark of laughter. His specialty had been—was—rheumatology, loosely translated as the study of going with the flow. It was probably time he started practicing what he preached. "Fine. When do you want to start experimenting?"

"A week Tuesday." Gemma clapped her hands excitedly. "Brilliant! You won't regret it. I promise."

"You're not including me in on this, are you?"

"You bet! You're top of the list. Look at your shoulders—tense as anything! Tension like that could lead to all sorts of spinal prob—"

Cole's phone rang and as he went to answer it he gave her an assenting nod. Of course he'd go. If it helped his clinicians it helped the clinic—which helped the patients. Gemma put the puppy down with a grin, melodramatically tiptoeing out of the office while mouthing an exaggerated "thank you".

He gave her a smile and a wave. She deserved it. Gemma was one of the clinic's true success stories. Originally a modern dancer, she had ripped just about everything you could in a knee and had come back fighting. Then had done it all over again. After a few dark months she'd rebounded, channeling the same passion she'd had for dance into dance rehabilitation and massage. She was looking at ticking osteopathy off her list if the word in the staffroom was anything to go by.

The phone rang again.

"Dr. Manning."

"Madame Tibold on the line for you." Cole smiled at the sound of Lina's voice and just as quickly shifted into work mode. He rarely had calls from the City of London Ballet's director, and now twice in one week? He'd done the favor and she wasn't one to make thank-you calls. Madame Tibold on the phone usually meant an injury. A big one.

"Thank you, Lina. Put her through, please."

Lina clicked off the line, her hand visibly shaking. She wondered if Madame Tibold had recognized her voice. The last words she had heard from the matriarch of the ballet corps had been, "It's a hard life and you gave it your best. Good luck in life, Lina. You'll need it."

The words had lacerated her heart. She had forsaken friendships, time with her family, schoolgirl crushes—everything a normal girl would've done with her free time—so that she could rehearse. Rehearse and take classes and train and stretch her feet and increase her arches. Everything! All she had worked toward her entire life had been that handful of lead roles, and at her darkest moment she'd been dismissed as if she'd been a pretender all along. At least, that was how it had felt. Particularly when the visits from her "friends" at the ballet had dried up pretty quickly after she'd left hospital.

That had been when she had realized just how alone she was. She'd all but trained her parents not to call.

"I'm too busy. Rehearsal."

"I can't even think about a visit for a few months, class is really intense right now."

She had let the few childhood friendships she'd had fall by the wayside, and as for friends in the ballet corps it was obvious now she hadn't really gone there. Her focus on getting to the top had been too intense. Maybe that's what Madame had been saying. *You've made your own crosses to bear—now let's see how you go about carrying them.*

It was the only way she had thought she could be the best. And now it was the only way she knew she could survive. Keeping her heart locked up tight.

"Lina, sorry to do this, but can you look after Igor for a bit?" Cole appeared in front of her desk, sending a ripple of goose pimples surging along her arms. Those blue eyes of his were mesmerizing. Best not to look into them too closely. Cole might be her knight in shining armor on the finance front—but that was as far as things would go. Now, as for the puppy... She reached out her arms and took hold of the furry critter.

"Of course." She glanced up at the wall clock. The clinic shut at six—looking after Igor until then shouldn't be too much of a bother. Never mind the fact that the only thing she'd vaguely mastered that day had been the telephone system. Turned out office work didn't come as naturally as she'd hoped.

"I'm not exactly sure when I'll be back—one of the guys has blown his knee out—but I'll ring you with an update." Cole shot her an apologetic grimace, then winked. "See you later?"

"Yes, of course, Dr. Manning."

What was up with the winking?

Her stomach did a flip-flop.

And what was up with the funny tummy? She didn't do flirting.

Did she?

"Thanks, Lina. And it's Cole when the patients aren't around, all right? See you later. The rest of Igor's things are in my office." Cole was out the door before she had a chance to stop him. She and Igor eyed one another. Dog-sitter hadn't really been part of the deal. Or had it? Good thing he was cute. The dog, that was. Not Cole. Well…

Lina scrunched one hand through her hair and stared into the puppy's eyes. There had to be an easier way to get herself out of debt, didn't there?

"OMG! You've got puppy time!" Gemma skidded to a halt in front of Lina's desk. She grinned. If that girl did anything in a speed other than double time, Lina would be amazed.

"Yes, well, Dr. Manning had to rush off and asked me to look after him until he was finished."

"Ooh, special treatment, eh?"

"If you consider pooper-scooper duty as special." Lina couldn't help but smile back. Gemma's positivity was contagious—and catching a bit of that sunny attitude would be good for her. She'd spent so much of her life being focused she didn't know if she'd ever been giddy outside performances. It was the only thing that had made her feel truly alive.

"Good point. He says he's going to give him up for adoption, but I doubt it. There's a big old heart lurking beneath that supermodel exterior." Gemma nodded her multicolored coif decisively, before abruptly changing her expression. "Hey, you wouldn't be interested in getting a free sports massage, would you?"

Lina stiffened instantly. She had only agreed to take the position here to get some money. Being "investigated" on a physical level was a whole other kettle of fish she didn't want to get into. On the other hand, she couldn't afford any massages and knew treatment could break down scar tissue, increase her flexibility and help her with a diminishing range of movement. But asking for help? She just wasn't there yet.

Gemma put her hands into the "pretty please" temple and pushed out her lower lip to make a sad clown face. "You'd be helping me heaps if you could come. Did I mention they were *free*? There will be a tiny bit of interaction between the other volunteers but nothing horrible. I super cross my heart promise!" And she did it for good measure.

Well. Gemma *had* shown her how to use the phones. One good turn and all that. Besides, what was the worst that could happen?

"It's gone."

"The whole thing?" Madame Tibold crossed her arms and gave Cole her famed wide-eyed stare. The one that brought the world's most famous ballerinas to tears.

"Do you want to tell him or shall I?"

Cole didn't even blink. After losing Katie, he'd had to plumb a huge reserve of professional cool he hadn't known he'd had. These days, he could take telling just about anyone anything. They were just facts. And you had to deal with them. How people dealt with them? That wasn't up to him.

"But he's had surgery before on the other knee. Surely, another would be easy enough—"

"I'm going to stop you there, Madame." Cole held up a hand. "Yes, Marc's had reconstructive surgery on the other knee and we can fix the cruciate ligament—but with both knees not entirely stable, it should be his choice how to proceed."

"Dancing is his life." Madame's ring-bedecked fingers moved to her hips.

"That's for him to say."

"He will choose to dance."

"Given half a chance, I'm sure Lina would've done the same."

Both Cole and Madame looked surprised to hear her name mentioned. Neither more so than Cole.

"Lina had an injury that wouldn't let her dance again. It was different." Madame's eyes betrayed a microwince of guilt.

"That's right. She didn't have a choice. Marc does. Let him make it."

Madame went to interject, but Cole raised a hand and calmly continued.

"There are numerous surgeries for a burst cruciate ligament. Shunts, supports, surgical tissue grafts. Auto- or allograft. We might need to use some of the hamstring, which would have a lead-on effect. Those are just a few of a number of excellent options *for a normal lifestyle*—but for a dancer? They're not the same as the real deal. I'm not trying to rain on your parade, or Marc's...but to dance again full-time? He has to be aware that he could destroy one or both of his knees permanently."

The pair of them stood there, arms crossed, each committed to their own stance. A tension of grudging respect crackled between them. To Cole it was a no-brainer. Choose life. Marc was young enough to make a career change now if he wanted.

Something inside him shifted. What if your life meant nothing without your true passion? Without your first love?

"Um...hello?" He turned at a tap on his shoulder.

"Lina! You found us. Excellent. Apologies." Cole scrubbed a hand along his head, his telltale time-buyer. "Thanks for coming over."

"Lina, how lovely to see you."

Cole watched as Lina's body went rigid and an expression of terror ripped across her face. Seeing Madame, it appeared, wasn't quite as lovely. It hadn't even crossed his mind to say that Madame Tibold would be at the hospital when he'd rung to see if Lina could bring Igor over.

"Bonsoir, madame." Lina's face was a picture of elegant restraint. Her greeting included a light smile and a curtsy, of course. Some habits were obviously hard to break.

Madame Tibold would be right at home at his parents' country club, from the looks of things. A place where charm and etiquette were far more important than the truth.

"Let me ask you." Madame Tibold wasted next to no time with niceties, fixing her dark eyes on Lina. "Do you think it's right that a renowned practitioner of dance rehabilitation would counsel a patient that they shouldn't dance again?"

"I—" Lina's eyes shot to Cole.

"I didn't say that," Cole interjected. He wouldn't be played. Not now. Not ever again. "I said it was Marc's *choice*. I can offer him the facts and the facts are—" He stopped himself, aware he'd been about to breach patient-doctor confidentiality.

"No, do go ahead," Madame intoned. "I am his

legal guardian. Have been for some time. You may speak freely."

"I don't need to be involved." Lina waved away any responsibility but found her arm restrained by Madame's aging fingers. From the look on Lina's face, it had happened before and had been just as unpleasant. Cole watched as the light drained from Lina's eyes.

"I just came to tell Dr. Manning that Gemma came over with me and is waiting outside with Igor. No dogs—even puppies—allowed in hospital, remember, Dr. Manning?"

"Do stay, dear. It'd be interesting to hear what someone with no career has to say about a doctor destroying a professional's future."

"No one is destroying anyone's future, Madame." Cole's eyes spit fire while his voice held caged restraint. "Marc's injuries are serious."

"And there are surgeries that can be done." The determined woman held her ground.

Cole shifted his feet and adopted a neutral tone. "Madame Tibold, I am going to have to ask you, respectfully, that we leave all decisions up to Marc. It's his body. It's his life and he's only seventeen. What he chooses now will impact his entire future." Cole's face was all business now. Any Southern charm he might have been using had turned into granite resolve. He knew how hard it was to accept someone's decision—even if it wasn't the same as his own—but he had taken an oath. And there wasn't a ballet director in the world who would get him to veer from it.

"Either way, he will be off stage *and* out of the rehearsal studio for many, many months. If he does his rehab and *if* he feels happy to continue, it should be left entirely up to him."

"I agree with Dr. Manning." Lina's voice broke into the strained atmosphere. "A dancer is also a person, Madame. And that person should be allowed to make a choice. Of course you know that I didn't have one."

"Lina. I didn't mean—"

"Yes, I think you did. If you'll excuse me?" It was less of a question and more of an announcement. At which point Lina turned on her heel and left as swiftly as she'd arrived. Cole was impressed. He couldn't imagine how much courage it had taken Lina to speak to Madame in that way. Perhaps knowing she would—could—never go back? She obviously didn't know Madame had made the initial call for Lina to be given an interview. Neither, thanks to her secrecy, would Lina ever know.

"So?" Madame gave Cole an approving once-over. "You got her to come out of hiding."

"That was her choice, Madame. Not mine."

"Oh...' Madame ran her eyes up and down him another time. "It seems to me when you want to be, you can be very persuasive. Too bad you don't choose to exercise that skill with your patients. Let's go and speak with Marc, shall we? Explain to him his options."

The elegant woman, who had clearly been a beauty in her day, hooked her thin hand into the crook of Cole's arm and gave him the go-ahead nod. They would do it Cole's way. This time.

CHAPTER FOUR

"How strong are the meds they have you on?"

From the dip and swoop of his eyelids, it was pretty clear that Marc was heavily loaded.

"Not strong enough," the young dancer muttered, clenching his eyes tightly against the pain.

Lina knew well enough how he felt. The pain wasn't just physical. He was living through his biggest fear. A time when it was impossible to believe there was any light at the end of the tunnel. She felt her own breath become restricted as she took in the scene. She didn't even dare look up at the ceiling. How many nights had she stared at a hospital ceiling? Too many. Too many to remember.

"Have they spoken with you yet?"

"Dr. Manning did for a bit," Marc answered, eyes still closed.

"And Madame did for a lot longer?" Lina guessed. Madame hadn't even come to hospital when she had shattered her ball joint. Just being here, smelling the weave of scents of the hospital, was beginning to twist and tighten her gut. The fact that Madame had been here meant there was hope for Marc. At least for a while. And Madame was renowned for getting the most from her "investments."

"Will it get any better? Not dancing?"

"Is that what they told you?" Lina sat bolt upright on her vinyl hospital chair. She wouldn't have wished what she'd been through on anyone.

"Not so much. But Dr. Manning just droned on and on about the facts."

"I think he wants you to know everything you can about your injury. There are so many different surgeries you need to choose from."

Was she standing up for Cole? Madame may not have been in the room, but speaking against her was akin to treason!

"So I should just get the surgery and dance as long as I can? *Dance! Dance!*" Emulating the melodramatic tones of Madame Tibold.

"But isn't that just obeying Madame Tibold?"

They eyed each other warily, then burst out into silent giggles, tears eventually popping into Lina's eyes she was laughing so hard. Madame Tibold could appear at any minute and hysterical laughter was hardly the thing they wanted her to hear.

"Stop! *Arrête!* Please, I can't shake my knee so much. I think I've invented new ways of destroying it."

Lina sobered in an instant. "I'm so sorry, Marc."

"It's not over, is it?" He looked all man, but sounded like a frightened boy. Dancing was what he had done since he was three and now he was looking at, very possibly, a series of reconstructive surgeries that may or may not leave him able to dance again.

"No." Lina shook her head slowly. "It's not all over. Dr. Manning is excellent and works with an incredible pool of rehab specialists. Listen to them. I didn't and I'm paying the price." She shook her head at her own foolishness. "I know it's hard to believe, but it seems there is this thing called life."

"*Dancing* is my life!" A tremble hit his voice at the end of his words.

"It was mine, too. And I know it doesn't feel like it..." Lina had to stop for a moment. Her voice had gone as wobbly as Marc's. The tears of laughter were now charged with sorrow and were threatening to flood her eyes. "You have a choice. I guess you have to decide how you want to live. How you would like your body to be. Just take some time to imagine what you would do if—if you absolutely couldn't dance again." Lina felt the wall she'd tried so hard to build in front of her feelings crumble. "If I can see the light at the end of the tunnel...I think anyone can."

"Really?" Marc's eyes filled with hope.

"Just... Oh... What do I know, Marc? Just don't let anyone tell you what to do. Dr. Manning is on your side whatever you choose, and Madame... You have to get the surgeries anyway, so...'

"So...I just wait and see." He gave a dissatisfied shrug.

"You have a choice," Lina pressed. It was more than she'd had. "You have a choice."

"And how do you do today, sir? What can we help you with?" Lina studied her patient for a moment, arms crossed, glasses balanced atop her pile of curls, her face the absolute picture of concentration.

"Oh? Is it your leg? No. Wait a minute. *Co*

można nazwać legbone? Femur? Femur. Is it your femur that is troubling you today, sir? Or should I say Master Igor?"

Cole couldn't hold back any longer. "Technically, it's a greenstick fracture—and, as you will no doubt discover, it's an injury more common in our younger patients. The more mature ones tend to just go all out for a full break—but a compound? Thankfully, those are rare in our line."

"Oh! Dr. Manning, I didn't hear you." Color flooded Lina's pale cheeks. She clapped her hands over them for good measure.

"Not to worry. And it's Cole!" He sat himself down on the bench where Lina had been giving Igor his "treatment" and gave the puppy a little scratch under the chin. When he turned to look at her again he was struck by her eyes, rimmed red.

His gut told him that was his fault. That he needed to fix it. Fold Lina into his arms and apologize for asking her to meet him here at the hospital. Not to mention the fact that the "rare" compounds he'd just mentioned were exactly what had taken her off the stage forever. Talk about open mouth, insert foot!

Still. He had to hand it to her. She was still at

the hospital—albeit outside the building—and talking shop with Igor to boot. A lesser person would have fled the scene. He had and it would eat away at him until the day he died.

"I think it's brilliant—what you're doing. I wish all our staff showed such dedication."

"Well, I— It's not too late, really, and it wasn't exactly as if I could just leave. Gemma couldn't hang around any longer and you did leave me in charge of Igor after all."

"Yes, but it wasn't meant to be for so long. After you left him I went in to see Marc again. He is going to take some time to weigh his options, *despite* Madame's look." He tried to mimic the look and eked just the hint of a smile from Lina.

"Madame will speak with him. She will win." A shadow crossed her face. Seeing her former employer had obviously had a bitter sting to it.

"Maybe. Maybe not. He's got me in his corner. And whatever you said clearly resonated with him."

Lina's lips pushed out into a frowny moue. "I didn't say much."

"You danced together, he said. And he respected

you. Respects you," he corrected, waiting for the words to sink in. "You have perspective."

"And this is why you were so long in coming to collect your dear, beloved Igor?" Lina redirected the conversation abruptly. From the look on her face, she didn't want to go there. Fair enough. He had plenty of things he never wanted to speak with anyone about. Ever.

"Yes, sorry. I guess I'm not used to being responsible for anyone else." As the words came out of his mouth he felt the irony. *He'd had responsibility for another life all right. And when the life-support system had been switched off, life as he'd known it had changed forever.*

He cleared his throat roughly and pointed at the dog to clarify—but as his hand fell back to his side, he knew he didn't just mean Igor. By bringing Lina into the En Pointe fold he had accepted responsibility for her, as well. Only this time his feelings weren't altogether...*professional.*

What was it he was going to do—practice going with the flow? Bend with the willow and all that?

"I wasn't going to leave." Her words were defensive.

"No, no. Of course not." He drummed the bench

next to him with his fingertips. "What do you say I make up for it in the form of a walk in the park for Igor and a killer ice-cream cone for you? There's an amazing Italian guy who's got a stand just at the edge of the park across from here."

Lina eyed him warily, which was only fair. He had already imposed on her evening. Well, her life really. She could always say no. But he really hoped she didn't.

"Or overtime. I owe you that. At the very least."

Lina took her time considering her options. Her brows crinkled together and her lips did a little wiggle back and forth as she thought. And then it hit him. He didn't want to say goodbye. Not just yet.

"How amazing is this ice cream?"

"Depends upon how much you like double chocolate gelato or salted caramel…'

"All right, Dr. Manning. Please may I have my overtime in the form of ice cream?"

"*Pyszne!* Delicious,' Lina translated.

Cole made a stab at pronouncing the Polish word and it was all Lina could do not to choke on her ice cream. He may have English covered—

but the man had a mountain to climb before he'd be bilingual.

"I think you'd better stick to medicine." She gave him a wry look, slipping her fingers into the gaps between the slats of the park bench to stop herself from giving him a playful swat.

"Stick with what you know and all that, right?"

"Something like that." Lina fell silent. She knew ballet and sticking with that was impossible now. She felt Cole's hand cover and squeeze hers but she didn't dare risk looking at him. The sting of tears was teasing at her nose and she'd already cried enough today. Cried enough for a lifetime.

"Poor choice of expression." He released her hand. "Do you want to talk about it?"

"Not particularly."

"Fair enough."

Lina snuck a glance at him. He wasn't pressing. It was nice. When she'd been in hospital it had seemed as though everyone—the doctors, nurses, visitors, her parents for the short time they'd been able to visit—had all pushed and prodded. How did she feel? Was she sad? Did she think she needed medication for any depression she might be having? Did she want to talk to anyone professional? No, no, no, no, *no*!

She hadn't wanted any of these things. She'd just wanted to dance. The impact of her injury had been so profound that when she'd finally walked—*hobbled* was more like it—out of the hospital, she had been completely and utterly numb.

She wouldn't tell him, but this job had brought her back from teetering on the edge of the abyss. It was hard to believe she had sunk so low she had nearly been homeless rather than go home to her parents. She just couldn't do that to them. So it was time to start listening to some of her own advice. Because of the job, she now had a choice. But how did you start your whole entire life over when the first twenty-seven years had been focused on one very specific thing?

"How'd you get on today?" Cole broke the silence.

"Fine."

"No hitches with the phone system thingy?"

Lina had to smile. Without Gemma's help she doubted she would've taken a single call the entire day. As it was, she'd been busy from start to finish, felt utterly exhausted, but had come out the other end. Just in time to see Madame Tibold. The last person she'd expected to see ever again. And the very same woman who'd steered her on the intense career trajectory to center stage.

Had her nerves jingled and jangled today? Most assuredly. But she'd faced the day and Madame. Proudly. Answering the phone was hardly on a par with brain surgery—but from the perspective of someone trying to leave the all-encompassing shroud of darkness behind, getting through a day of work felt good.

"I did all right."

"Modest."

"It's pretty easy to pick up." *Some of it. Definitely not all of it.*

"And you're finding interacting with the patients okay?"

Easier than she'd thought. It was less "them" and more "I know what you're going through." That had surprised her.

"Yes, of course."

"The chair?"

"Comfy. Now stop interrogating me!" She took a lick of her ice-cream cone and settled back onto the bench. The park was nice. She'd never been there before. Dogs, it turned out, were an excellent means of discovering a city's green spots. Honestly? She didn't know if she'd ever just sat in the park before. With an ice-cream cone.

And a man whose mere presence made her a little closer to behaving like a giggly girlie than she'd care to admit.

"How was your day at work?" She only just stopped herself from adding a "dear' to the end of her question.

"Ah—I see what you're doing. Turning the tables?"

"I am merely showing an interest in the clinic's clients."

Cole laughed good-naturedly. "Well, that's good, then. I'm pleased we haven't put you off. I was nervous it was your way of getting me to talk about myself."

"Why? What's so bad about you?"

"Other than my inability to keep time, lumber people with puppies they didn't ask for and a weakness for ice cream?"

"The last thing isn't so bad." She took a dramatic lick of her cone and ended up with some on the tip of her nose.

"Don't they teach you how to eat ice cream cones in Poland?" Cole dabbed away the smear with a serviette and paused for just a moment, his eyes locking with hers.

Lina's breath caught in her throat. Was Cole going to kiss her? She felt her body go hot and cold all at once. *What am I going to do now?*

"I hear they have much more practice of ice-cream cones in America." Could he hear the wobble in her voice?

"What? You're not going down the route of saying all Americans have some weight to lose, are you?"

Lina stopped herself from making a lingering appraisal of him.

"I'm not saying that at all. But since life in America is supposed to be so nice, why did you come here?"

"Oh—you know...I needed...change."

"What? From your secret life as an ice-cream critic?"

"Something like that."

And that's when she saw it. The hit of grief

shadowing the bright blue of his eyes. It surprised her how much it affected her to see him in pain. He'd been nothing but a lift to her and to see him struggling with something of his own? It was hard to imagine anything that would get Cole Manning down.

Cole finished his cone with a flourish and smiling widely, pressed his hands down onto the bench, raising his lower body off the bench planks whilst lifting his legs into a half pike. *Interesting.* He wasn't bulky, but he surely had to work out to exercise that sort of muscle control. He must have abs to die for! Running a finger or two along those would be— *Uh, whoopsy! Stop the bus!*

Lina realigned her gaze to the remains of her dark-chocolate-and-salted-caramel double-scoop cone. Visually undressing Cole wasn't part of the plan. Not that there was a plan.

"I know I said I'd give you a week to figure out if you wanted to stay, but is it too soon to ask if you're up for a three-month trial period?"

Lina turned to face Cole, who had just scooped Igor up into his lap. The two of them looked at her expectantly. Igor's ears were pricked up and Cole's blue eyes were… *Mmm…* She might be imagining things, but Cole's eyes seemed to hold the promise of kindness, a gentle touch when it came to confronting her demons… He wouldn't push her, his eyes said. He'd just be there. And right now that seemed good enough. Good enough to stay awhile.

It was the biggest room in En Pointe and already it was full to bursting. Lina casually sidled toward the door. Gemma obviously had enough guinea pigs for her massage night—it would be easy enough to slip out with no one being any the wiser.

"And where do you think you're going?" A familiar chest blocked the doorway. If she looked straight up she knew she'd be looking directly into the blue eyes she'd been tactically avoiding for the past fortnight.

"Nowhere?" Lina hadn't meant for it to be a question, or for it to be addressed to his chest, but Cole's presence played havoc with any cool or calm she had shored up—so best to go with it. She widened her eyes for effect and shrugged her shoulders up tight round her ears.

"Exactly right. If I'm stuck, you're stuck."

"Oh, I think there are enough—"

"Uh-uh! No, you don't." Cole blocked the doorway with his arms and nodded toward the far end of the room where Gemma was clambering onto a chair. Lina turned around, grateful for the respite from those eyes. And his freckles. She'd never noticed before that he had a little smattering of freckles. Cute.

No!

Not cute. Definitely not cute. Authoritative. Well…and we're back to cute. *Turn around!*

"Okay, everyone, it turns out we've had more of you show up for massages than we have trainee masseurs, so what we're going to do is teach you all to massage each other! Yippee! Today is all about shoulders." Gemma's ability to control a group with a grin and a brisk clap of the hands was admirable. "Everybody pick a partner!"

Lina stiffened. She couldn't help it. Coming along to the sports massage session was a big enough step for her but today had been a particularly active one and she really could have done with going home and having a good soak complete with a fluffy cloud of bubbles floating up to the rim of her bath. The pepper-scented kind that gave her hip the illusion of feeling better. Healing. It'd been two weeks since she'd started at En Pointe, but the learning curve was still steep and she was nowhere near crossing the emotional bridge into the comfort zone.

"Guess that leaves you and me, Lina. It seems no one wants to feel my healing touch." Cole appeared at Lina's side with a self-effacing smile. "Feeling up to kneading the knots out of my shoulders?"

Uh…not even remotely!

"Sure. Why not? You look stiff as a plank."

"I guess that's better than being as thick as two short ones." Cole threw back his head and laughed.

Little speckles of heat tickled at her cheeks. Her English must've failed her again. Cole seemed to be having that effect on her.

"Lina! Cole! You two are over here on the floor, I'm afraid. We're out of massage chairs."

"We seem to be drawing all the short straws today, eh, Lina?"

"Thanks a lot."

"I didn't mean you, Polly Pigtails!" Cole's mock-pained expression brought a smile to her face as her hands flew to clutch her two thick plaits protectively. She drew them up into little U shapes and put on her best bucktoothed smile.

Her smile broadened with his. She couldn't help it. Hadn't been able to for the past two weeks now. Cole in the room meant a smile on her face. It was almost as though she'd been frozen for the months following her accident and his warm demeanor was bringing about a longed-for thaw. It was easier to think it had been his puppy—which he still hadn't managed to rehome—but Igor was nowhere in sight and here she was, grinning from ear to ear.

"Me first!" Cole dropped to his knees in front of her. "I've been up to my eyeballs in paperwork today and sources say I could do with a good old shoulder rub." He threw her another one of those over-the-shoulder winks of his. She'd seen him do it to other people—an upward shift of the chin, the casual descent of his eyelid, just briefly eclipsing the pure sky blue of his eyes… Not that she'd paid that much attention. Not really. He did it all the time, right? So, it was obvious that being on the receiving end of one wasn't special—but it had been harder to stem the rush of butterflies each of those leisurely winks unleashed. And now she was going to have to massage him? *Niebo mi pomoc.* And just how, exactly, could heaven help her?

"Shirts on or off?"

Lina's stomach lurched. Then did a cartwheel. Then lurched again. Cole was her boss. She didn't need to be rubbing his well-oiled, seminaked body in front of—

"On, you cad! This is a place of work! The boss doesn't stand for silly talk!" Gemma's words brought a wash of emotion to Lina's throat. *Mixed feelings? That would be one way to put it.* She needed this job. Big-time. It had only been a couple of weeks but already it was giving her some longed-for structure, purpose and, in truth, opening her eyes to a whole series of physio and treatment therapies she hadn't known existed. Maybe one day she'd see if someone could help her with her hip. Perhaps even take up Cole on his offer to go over her file. One day. But not today and definitely not now with that please-help-me-I-need-you look on his face.

Giving Cole a massage would move their working relationship—which was about as hands-off as you could get—to a whole different terrain. Intimate terrain. And with his shirt off? She could only just imagine the—

"Is something wrong?" Cole's face looked as though she'd just sprouted a moustache.

"What? No. Why?" The words tumbled out as heat began to crawl along her cheeks again.

"Because you look like you're poised to attack a huge, smelly pile of pumpernickel dough, not give your boss a little life-affirming shoulder rub."

"How dare you compare yourself to pumpernickel? It's delicious!" Not to mention the dough being a near match to the warm caramel color of his skin.

"And I'm not?" Cole's eyes sparked, his chin upright, expectant as he waited for an answer. "Wait. No. I take that back. Don't answer on the grounds it might incriminate you. Or both of us."

The space between them seemed to disappear—as if the air were actively binding them together. Lina knew in an instant what she felt for Cole was more than the gratitude of someone who needed a job. From the moment she'd first laid eyes on him it was as if he'd waved a magic wand and turned her world from black and white to Technicolor. With him, she felt safe, like she was in a Cole-and-Lina-sized superbubble of protection. But was she trapping herself in another fantasy?

Pouring herself into something wasn't new. Giving herself entirely to the ballet had yielded nothing but heartbreak. Would giving herself to the dream of a bright future—one with Cole in it—be just as foolish?

"Right, everyone." Gemma clapped her hands sharply, instantly breaking the fizzing connection between them. "If the person giving the massage could just rub their hands together briskly so as not to put icy digits onto their partner's necks."

Lina followed the instructions in a daze. If she treated this like a rehearsal, the rehearsal of a woman pretending she wasn't the least bit affected by placing her hands along the neck of her lover—*Aaaaiiiiieeee! Where did that come from?* She and Cole had barely breached the friendship zone, let alone something that intimate. And yet…she became aware of her hands fluidly massaging the length of Cole's neck, shifting down along the curve toward his shoulders, fingers pressing into muscle—some tight, some not—and she watched as Cole responded to her touch, his body pressing into the rhythmic cadence of her hands...

"All right, everybody! Looks as though some of you have your groove on. Sorry to bust it up, but it's time to switch places!"

Lina rose in synchronicity with Cole and as he turned she felt his hand brush against hers—their eyes meeting simultaneously. Did he feel the same electric connection she did? Was his heart pounding as rapidly as her own? Would she ever tire of even just a glimpse of his unbearably blue eyes?

Sitting down and facing the wall seemed to be the best way to quell the ricocheting emotions turning her insides into a pinball machine. She crossed her legs, took in a deep breath and smiled a little as she heard him do the same. Just maybe he had felt the same complex rush of response to her touch.

And then Cole's hands were on her shoulders. The warmth they transmitted merged into her skin like a yearned-for tonic. His fingers smoothed along her neck, each hand—one by one—shifting her plaits to the front of her shoulders. A hand cupping the side of her head as his fingers soothed the length of her neck into something long and fluid. Her body responded to him as it would have if they had been dancing. One touch eliciting another movement, each connecting to the other as if they had known the choreography all along. Her breath quickened as Cole increased the intensity of pressure he had been using. An impulse to turn around and kiss him, taste his lips, touch his skin, even caress him threatened to overwhelm her.

Abruptly, Lina grabbed her jumper from the floor and pushed herself up to standing.

"I'm sorry. I—I just remembered, I am late for something."

"What? Lina, what's going on?" Cole was straight behind her as she sought refuge in the corridor.

"No, it's just…" Her hands moved automatically to her shoulders, giving warmth to the area his hands had just left. She couldn't do it. Not here. Not in front of everyone. Cole's touch elicited too much raw feeling.

"It was a shoulder massage, Lina." Cole reached out and gave her arm a quick squeeze. "Nothing more."

"I know." She was holding back tears now. Tears of embarrassment, shame, confusion. She just needed to get out of there. Away from Cole and all the feelings he seemed to be able to tap into like some sort of emotion diviner.

"It's been a while, hasn't it?" He dipped his head down so they were eye to eye. It was near impossible not to look away.

"Since what?"

"Since you've let yourself be touched. Held."

How did eyes carry so much *compassion* in them? Biting the insides of her cheeks only just kept the tears from spilling over.

Lacing his fingers through hers, he silently led her to his office. As the door shut behind them, she was aware of nothing but being folded into Cole's arms. Her forehead pressed against his chest and her hands pushed. Hard. But he held her to him until the fight in her began to ebb away. And that's when the tears began to flow in earnest. The logjam of emotion she had been holding back for months, if not years, had broken. The heartbreak, the pain of the surgeries, the bleeding feet, all of the missed birthdays, anniversaries, quiet moments with her family. The debt of time, money, sheer devotion she owed her parents, the endless flow of wishes that she had the ability to pay them back for an infinity of kindness—the fathomless depth of their love and belief in her... All of it whooshed up and poured out of her in a heated wash of tears, all of them cleansing.

And he stayed with her. Listened to her sob, let her use his shirt as a tissue over and over as each time she thought she was done and she looked up into those blue eyes of his, the tears began anew.

This wasn't new for Cole. Something in treatment giving a patient release. But the churn of emotion he was experiencing was new. More than anything, he wanted Lina to know she would be safe. Safe, right here in his arms. He looked up to the ceiling and gave it a wry smile. For now.

He had nothing to offer her long-term. Or short-term, for that matter. He had nothing to offer her.

Even so, just having his arms around her, holding her close to him, was one of the most natural things he had ever experienced. There wasn't a person in the world she'd felt she could go to and—after a bit of a fight—she'd stayed with him, opened the door just one small crack. Would it be fair to try and get her to open it a bit further?

Cole let his chin rest on Lina's head as her sobs slowed into deep, hiccupy breaths.

"Better?"

"Mmm." The murmur came from where she'd nestled into his chest. He turned his head so that his cheek rested on her head. If anyone were to walk in right now they would assume they were lovers. Soul mates. He pushed the thought aside and forced himself to focus on her.

"Anything you want to talk about?"

It's still too painful to talk about.

"No."

Surprise, surprise.

"I am a doctor, you know."

"Not my doctor."

"True, but if you want, I can help." He laughed good-naturedly. "Don't look at me so dubiously! I worked long and hard to get my medical degree. My parents made sure of it." He pulled back a bit and his voice turned sober. "I wasn't offering to be your shrink, but if there's anything I can do for you—take a look at your records or anything…"

"I don't want a doctor." She looked up at him, her green eyes still glassy with tears.

What was she saying exactly? Did she want *him*? Cole minus the protective medical accolades and folksy charm? Plain old Cole who made bad choices? Cole Manning who'd pulled the plug on his fiancée despite the heartbreak, not just for him but for both his and her parents? He didn't know if that Cole would be worth much to Lina. It hadn't been to his parents. Or Katie's. Or the rest of his hometown for that matter. Folk stuck together when they thought a wrong had been done. Obeying a DNR apparently didn't fall into the "right' category. And who could blame them? It had been the hardest thing he'd ever done.

"Well…I guess that puts us at a bit of an impasse."

Her brow lifted a fraction.

"You don't like to accept help and I don't like to interfere in other people's lives." He held her out at arm's length, making a show of sizing her up. "Maybe it's perfect. We were made for each other!" He flashed her his best cheesy salesman smile. It was the best he could muster after the dredging up of the past.

"That attitude doesn't sound very generous for a doctor." Lina wriggled out of his arms as if to punctuate her point, and he couldn't help feel the sting of disappointment.

"That's not true." He hadn't meant for his tone

to be sharp, but if anyone had done some deep soul-searching, it was him. And he knew exactly how he stood as a doctor. "I give every patient one hundred percent. They get the best advice I can possibly offer—but at the end of the day that's all it is. The work, the passion, the commitment? I can't give them that. That's got to come from within."

"Don't you think you're the reason patients work hard?"

"No. Why should I?" He led her over to the small sofa tucked into his office's bay window and handed her a box of tissues just in case. "I'm not the one who has the work ahead of me. What if I were to sit here and say to you, you know—having this accident could have been the best thing that ever happened to you."

She pulled a face. Then reconsidered.

I never would have met you.

"I can see you're not persuaded."

Cole checked an urge to give Lina's shoulder a gentle knead. Being the boss meant reining in any attraction he felt. So squelch it down he did.

"Look. I have no idea what you're going through and I can see how working here—with the dancers, the therapists, the injuries—has got to be taking a bit of a toll. You've gone from what I understand was a lot of alone time to full immersion back into the 'real world.' It's got to be tough and—believe me—I take my hat off to you. Not everyone could be as cheerful in the face of adversity."

A tear snaked down her cheek.

"Well. Mostly cheerful." He used the pad of his thumb to wipe it away, resisting the temptation to cup her face in his hand, run the backs of his fingers along her cheek. "Have you considered going home at all? To Poland?"

"No."

The sharpness of her response startled them both.

She hurriedly continued, "I mean, obviously, I love my parents—"

"But—what am I missing?"

"I will not go home. Not now." Her jaw set so tightly he saw a nerve twitch.

"Is there a 'when' lurking out there anywhere?" Even his best smile couldn't elicit a hint of the same from Lina.

"What do you want from me?" Every defense

she'd let down was re-erected in an instant. Walls double-thick this time.

"Well, I…" Cole stopped. This was not one of those moments to mess up. He thought of how proud he'd hoped his parents would be of their doctor son—and how he'd only brought them sorrow. Logical or not, he hadn't been able to stick around burdened by so much shame.

Could she feel the same?

Lina's face was creased with worry, upper teeth steadily catching her lower lip again and again, turning it a deep raspberry red. Did she only see him as another person to add to the list of people to disappoint?

"I wondered if you would consider going halves with me in taking Igor to puppy classes."

"I'm sorry?" She swiped at her tearstained face and grabbed her plaits, as if for comfort.

"Igor. I can't seem to find him a new home…" He stopped, gave a self-effacing grimace and corrected himself. "I'm finding it hard to say goodbye to the little fellow and now that his leg is better the very least I can do is send him to comportment classes. The thing is, the only one I can find that starts straight away is on a Wednesday and I can't make the first half-hour because of commitments at the hospital. If I were to give you overtime, would you be willing to take him? It's not far from here. Just the other side of the park, actually."

"No ice-cream payments?"

Was that the hint of a smile?

"That could always be arranged." He crossed his arms, giving her his best studied look. "Pending, of course, your success—and Igor's—at class."

Lina pushed herself up out the corner of the sofa, already tying on the mantle of a new challenge. "You're not suggesting Igor and I will let you down?"

"Far from it."

Far from it indeed. Cole actually felt her smile touch his heart this time. He couldn't put his finger on what barrier they'd broken through, but whatever emotional journey they seemed to be on, they were doing it together. And for the first time in an awfully long time it felt right—*real*—to have someone he could tuck protectively under his wing—even if only for a while.

CHAPTER FIVE

"AND THE PRIZE goes to…Igor and Lina!"

Lina knew she shouldn't, but the whoop was out of her mouth before she could stop it, hands clapping along with sheer glee. She hadn't felt this proud in ages. Proud of Igor, of course, but proud of herself, as well. They had focused and practiced and now they were at the head of the class! So what if it was for best sitting? She was well trained in the art of posture and could assert with absolutely assurance that Igor was following in her footsteps. His posture was immaculate. Nureyev would've been proud.

"Someone looks happy!" The voice she'd come to think of as Hot Chocolate Deluxe swirled along her spine. The expected bolt of heat detonated in her chest as she turned and met that bright blue set of eyes. She felt intimate and shy all at once. But mostly proud.

"Igor's been amazing today. He has real panache."

"So you two'll be showing off at Crufts next year?"

Lina swatted away the compliment. "Igor maybe. You won't get me running around a ring in front of thousands of people." The words were out almost before she'd thought them. It had been weeks since she'd used her cane. She wondered if running was out of the picture. It would be nice to start getting some proper exercise. Break a sweat and feel the afterglow of endorphins a good workout brought with it.

"I don't see why not. It'd be a lovely sight." Cole was scooping up Igor but finished up his pronouncement with his eyes fully locked with hers.

A little thrill of pleasure made her heart hitch. Gemma had egged her into coming along for a couple of gratis sports massages from her trainee students and she was definitely feeling better. Professional ballet might be off the agenda, but cycling? Running? They were all possibilities.

"Ice cream o'clock?"

"Yes, of course." Lina picked up her sweater and handbag, suddenly aware of a hit of nostalgia as her mind reeled through the well-studied menu. "The Italian flavors are lovely but, you know, it's really too bad they don't have beetroot with poppy seeds. And a sour-cream swirl. Ooh!" She couldn't stop herself from giving a twirl at the thought. "It's so good."

"Now, I can get you on the sour-cream front, but beets? I'm not buying it, Keminsky."

"It's very popular in Poland."

Cole's face registered disbelief.

"Well. Polish people eat it anyway. Lots. I am sure they have it at the Polski center."

"Where's that?"

"Near the river in Hammersmith. I used to go there—" She stopped, on the brink of admitting she'd felt more than a little homesick lately. After The Great Weep she was definitely feeling she could speak more freely to Cole—but "the home-run topics," as he liked to call them? Still too fresh.

"Why don't we go there now? We can jump in a cab." Cole was already heading toward the curb, arm raised as traffic approached.

"No. No—it's not necessary. I was just dreaming a little."

"I think after today's impressive show at puppy class you deserve to have a dream come true." He raised his arm again, this time bringing a taxi to a halt. "Where was it you said we were going?"

"Polskie Centrum Kultury—the Polish Cultural Centre," she said to the driver along with the address. He signaled for them to hop in the back of the black cab.

Settling into the seat, Lina couldn't stop a big grin from forming. One of her favorite things in Britain was the classic black cab and one of her favorite things from Poland was beetroot ice cream. She didn't feel ready to go home yet—but being at the cultural center always felt like stepping into a little section of Poland. Cole reached over and gave her hand a squeeze, then wrapped his fingers through hers.

"You look about five years old."

"I feel about five years old!" She squeezed his hand back and, despite her best intentions, kept her fingers laced through his. "Ice cream from home!"

They rode like that, in silence. Two people holding hands, heading off for some ice cream with their prizewinning pooch. It was amazing to feel so *happy*. An uncomplicated happy. Just good old-fashioned happy. Not to mention the little ideas that kept popping into her head. Maybe she could run. Maybe she could ride a bike. Maybe what she'd needed all along was not even a push, but the suggestion of a push. Perhaps what she'd needed all along was a certain someone who gave her the strength to believe in herself again.

She stole a glance at Cole, who was busy examining Igor's new prize. It was the third time he'd won Top Puppy and his toy collection was becoming enviable. Her gaze shifted along Cole's face. The long-lashed blue eyes, caramel skin darkening as the spring months became more summery… How could a man with such an open heart be so very single? He worked a lot and, if office gossip was anything to go by, dated but had never been known to have a girlfriend. Which was crazy. He was definitely a catch. If the way he made her feel was anything to go by, someone would be a very lucky woman someday.

He was very rigid about how he treated patients. They could take his advice or leave it. He was adamant that it wasn't up to him to make a patient's decision about their health. Some people

ANNIE O'NEIL

may have found that off-putting. Too scientific. But she liked it. He was right. If you didn't accept responsibility for yourself, who would?

She smiled down at their hands, still lightly clasped. Had she ever had anything near a normal boyfriend-girlfriend relationship before? She thought this was what it must be like. Feeling content. Light. Free.

Cole had passed the point of being able to hide his true feelings. Beetroot ice cream wasn't for him. Not by a long shot.

"They got any other flavors in there?"

"Honey and garlic?"

"You're joking, right?"

Lina shook her head in slow motion. It looked like nothing in the world would take the smile off her face, and he felt a tug of pride at having been a part of it. "I think they have the names in English somewhere—but I'm pretty sure there is sweet fish."

Cole looked appalled.

"No? Okay—watermelon?"

"Watermelon! Finally, something I can recognize. You Poles definitely have a—er—more refined palate than I do." A thought took hold and he nodded his head decisively. "One of these nights I'm taking you to a Southern food restaurant. I'd love to see how you get on with grits and blackened catfish."

"Why would you put black on a catfish?"

"Ha! Don't curl your lip like that! It's the seasoning—it turns the fish black when it's cooked. Barbecued is best. With collard greens and a side of po'boys? Delicious!" He smacked his lips at the thought. His father made a mean blackened catfish on the grill and with a serving of his mother's fried green tomatoes? "It's delicious, you'll see." Cole didn't even think. He just swung his arm round the back of the bench and pulled Lina close to him for a quick squeeze. He only just managed to stop himself from giving her a peck on the cheek, opting to plop his arm on the back of the bench instead, not quite ready to take it away. Not just yet, because what was happening between Lina and him felt…good…regular, but in the absolute best way. He hadn't had "good" or "regular" in he didn't know how long. It had always been cotillions or daughters of couples from the country club, or the rotary club, or—

It just didn't matter because the whole town had always seemed to know whom Justin and Jenna Manning's son had had on his arm because they'd organized to get her there. Until "that night" with their best friend's daughter. He tightened his lips and flinched it away.

Right now? He was just a regular guy on a regular date with his girl and their dog. Except it wasn't a date and the only thing that was "his" was the dog.

"Hey, look, they are setting up a band." Lina nodded to the opposite corner of the quadrangle at the heart of the community center. Several older gentlemen—wearing suit jackets and ties despite the warmth of the early evening—were putting stools into place. One had an accordion, another a fiddle, a third was lugging a double bass into place.

"What's that?" Cole pointed toward a man carrying an unfamiliar instrument, noticing Lina's eyes brighten at his arrival.

"Ah—the *dudy* or *koza*. I am not sure exactly which one—they are regional—but it is like your Scottish bagpipes."

"They aren't *my* bagpipes!" Cole snorted. "I'm

American, remember? Apple pie and electric guitars and all that?"

"Yes, but..." Lina paused, her face a picture of concentration.

"What?" Cole gave her a little poke with Igor's paw to speed up her response.

"It's funny. I was just thinking how I always consider myself as the only one who is away from home in London—but I guess I'm not so alone in being alone, am I?"

"No," Cole answered easily, then, as their eyes met, he felt his response shift. There was more there. Something weighted with meaning. "No, you're not alone." He searched her pale green eyes, hoping more than anything that Lina knew he'd do what he could to stem any loneliness she felt. He'd actively sought the anonymity of big-city life, but he knew exactly what she was saying.

Sometimes it felt as though he was a natural part of the place, easily absorbed into the fray of the capital's population, just one of the millions of Londoners going about his business... And other days? Other days it felt like everything "foreign" about Britain was there to actively remind him he didn't have a home. He didn't have a place—

people—he could go to when he was hurting. He didn't have a "someone."

But being part of a person's life—laying himself open to all the hurt and anguish that went with loving them—he wasn't even close to being there yet. Might never be. If he'd been a man who prayed, right now he'd be sending a stream of prayers straight to heaven in the hopes Lina could see he was trying his best to do what he could. He stole a glimpse at her and smiled. She pushed herself to the edge of the bench, fingers curled round the edge of the seat, eyes bright with anticipation.

How could he not at least try? Spending time with Lina was evolving into something beyond a work relationship for him—but how much more? Shaking his head, he looked away. Answering that question was somewhere he couldn't go. Not by a long shot. Never mind the fact it wasn't fair on Lina. She was an employee, which made her strictly off-limits in the first place, and she was obviously busy battling her own demons. He pulled his hand back to his lap, where Igor was settling in for a nap. He'd be better sticking with "man's best friend."

The musicians began to play and couples drifted

to the center of the square and with a touch of the hand, or a fleeting caress on the cheek, they separated into individual lines of men and women, then began to dance. Their movements reminded him of the dances his parents used to drag him to where—despite himself—he'd usually ended up having a great time. It had been about family, community, not just swirling in long-rehearsed circles round one another. From the smiles on everyone's faces they, too, were reminded of better times at home.

"What is this?"

"The *kujawiak*. It's a national dance of Poland." Lina smiled at a private memory. "The first dance I learned. You learn it at school, you learn it in your village square, in your grandmother's kitchen. No matter what, if you are Polish you cannot escape the *kujawiak*."

"Show me?" Cole held out a hand. Just because she was an employee it didn't mean they couldn't share a dance.

"Hmm." Lina began shaking her head, her hand automatically reaching for her cane.

"No way. You can't use that as an excuse." Cole waved it away. "I've been watching you the past few weeks and you've hardly used it. I'm not even sure why you bring that thing with you anymore, to be honest."

"Yes, but I am not so sure…with the dancing."

Ah.

"Lina, look at these people. Everyone out there is about fifty years older than either of us and they're doing fine." He shifted Igor to the ground and swiftly fastened his lead to the bench. "C'mon, I bet there are at least four or five hip replacements out there." He tipped his head toward the dancers, who were slowly circling one another to the rhythm of the music.

Lina gave him a wary look but he could tell she was wavering. "Please? Would you do me the honor of dancing the *kujawiak* with me?" Lina stifled a giggle. "At the very least you can teach me the dance as we both know I'll never be able to pronounce it properly!"

"Go on, dear." An older woman good-naturedly nudged Lina with her elbow, speaking in Polish. "Don't turn down such a handsome fellow! You're obviously mad about each other. I'll look after your dog while I rest."

Lina rose, cheeks coloring as she did. She hadn't

thought the looks she'd shared with Cole had been so obvious. Then again...did that mean her feelings weren't one-sided?

Before she could reconsider, the woman slipped into her spot on the bench and tipped her head back into the final rays of the evening sun, eyes closed against the light. Lina couldn't help noticing that the woman looked a bit pale—but everyone in England looked a bit pale this time of year. It was probably nothing.

Cole offered her his hand. As she slipped her fingers across his palm it was all but impossible to hide her body's response to him. An overwhelming urge to arch in toward him took hold of her. She wanted to feel his chest against her own. Rise up on tiptoe and see if his lips tasted as nice as they looked. He clasped her hand in his and gave her arm a little tug, for which he received a shy smile as they moved into the square of dancers. If only he knew the saucy thoughts dancing round her head...with some fairy-tale thoughts latched on for good measure.

Everything about the evening felt like a first date. The ice cream, the hand squeezes, the short but, oh, so lovely moment when he'd slipped his arm across her shoulders. Even when Cole had moved it away to the back of the bench she'd still been able to feel the heated dance of goose pimples tickle their way up and down her spine. It would have been more than easy to snuggle right up, scoop Igor onto her lap and watch the dancers. Just a couple of young lovers— *Eek!*

Stop. Thinking. That. Word!

"So…where should I put my hands?"

Don't answer honestly!

"Just hold my right hand up like this and then…" Lina had to stop, it was too flustering, which was rich coming from a lifelong dancer. This was what she had done all day, every day for her entire adult life but right here, right now, with a man she could so easily imagine kissing that it suddenly seemed impossible.

"Don't you remember?" Cole laughed.

"Of course, it's just—it's been a while." She turned in a semicircle, ending up with her back to him, in sync with the other dancers. *See? It was all there.* Just like getting back on a bike. She pulled one of Cole's hands over her shoulders so that their fingers just met and signaled to him to watch the other male dancers. It was a simple enough dance. She'd been doing it in the school playground to the discordant accompaniment of teenaged musicians from the age of five. But it had never felt sexy before.

As Cole watched and mimicked, his movements became more fluid, more confident, and it was impossible not to respond to his touch. He lifted the tips of Lina's fingers up in a high arc and she spun in a slow circle before coming round to face him. The music was slow and crept into her bloodstream like a warm tonic. It reminded her of everything that had been familiar to her as a young girl. Experiencing it whilst being held in Cole's arms—slowly drifting this way and that in union with the dozen or so other couples—was little short of magic.

Their eyes locked and it was all Lina could do to remember to breathe. She felt Cole's hand tug her in a bit closer at the waist, his other hand teasing hers toward his chest. He slipped her fingers from his palm and laid them against his chest, his heartbeat palpable through the thick cotton fabric of his shirt. It was all Lina could do not to press herself into that chest as she had done the day she'd wept in front of him, but this time revel in his scent, the solidness of him—in both character and physicality. She had no idea if there was a washboard stomach under there but, frankly, right now? He could have a potbelly for all she cared. Being with Cole mattered to her. Mattered in a way she hadn't experienced before. And dancing here at the Polish Centre with him felt so incredibly *personal*.

It was as if, through their time at the clinic, sharing duties with Igor and now giving him this glimpse into her heritage, she was slowly opening the doors to plain old Lina. The Lina who had been inside her all along, but who she'd had to hide away so that she could focus on her career. She braved a glance up toward his face, happy to see a peaceful smile lazily playing on his lips. If Cole were to hold her like this, and they could sway back and forth to the music of her homeland forever? That would be enough. That would definitely be enough.

Abruptly Cole pulled back from their embrace. "Lina, over on the bench, by Igor..."

Adrenaline racing, she whirled round to see the woman who had encouraged her to dance slumped on the bench, Igor anxiously patting at her with a paw.

Cole was by the woman's side in an instant, fingers on her pulse points, a cheek by her mouth to check for breathing. "She's breathing, but we've got find out why she fainted."

Vaguely aware of the music coming to a stop and the dancers gathering round, Lina fine-tuned her focus on Cole.

"Can you help me lay her on the ground, please?" He was all business, pure concentration. He threw his jacket on the ground but then, with a quick look at Lina and a glance at the other woman's more generous proportions, thought better of it and suggested, "Maybe you could ask a couple of people to help us?"

Lina found herself playing the role of translator as the crowd around them closed in. Most people spoke English, as well, but not all of the older ones and here, where she knew everyone but Cole would understand, it was much easier to use her native tongue.

She hadn't spoken Polish with others in so long that had it not been an emergency she would have reveled in the pleasure of it. But from the ques-

tions Cole was throwing to her to ask the crowd—
Does anyone know this woman? Does she have
a handbag? Can we check for any medication?—
she knew time was of the essence. As they eased
the woman to the ground, she came to, muttering
a few words in Polish. She pressed her hands to
the ground as if to get up, then began shaking, a
thick patina of sweat appearing on her forehead.

"She says she needs something sweet."

Cole's eyes lit up with recognition.

"She must be diabetic. Can you ask someone to
grab an ice cream or a chocolate bar—anything?
She could be going into insulin shock." Lina nodded and rattled off the request.

The moments passed with excruciating slowness. Lina knelt on the ground, holding the woman
in a semiupright position. Her eyes went wide as
the woman began to twitch and spasm uncon-
trollably. Lina went with her gut instinct, wrapping her arms around the woman as tightly as she
could manage.

"She's seizing. The brain's not getting enough
glucose," Cole explained, quickly placing several
rolled-up serviettes left over from their ice cream
between the woman's teeth.

Lina called for someone to ring an ambulance just as a young man handed across a large green handbag that must have been on the far side of the bench. He grabbed hold of the woman's legs to help control her shaking as Cole unceremoniously dumped the contents of the woman's handbag onto the ground.

"It's too late for the ice cream. Let me see if she has any glucagon in here."

He raked through the usual items—coin purse, public transport pass, house keys, tissues—until he unearthed a small orange plastic box. Inside was a syringe and small glass bottle topped with an orange lid. The vial looked like it held a small disc of powder.

Cole bit off the lid of the syringe and as he injected the liquid from the syringe into the vial, Lina asked another man to hold the woman's legs, her eyes still trained on Cole. "What are you doing?"

"I'm hydrating the glucagon powder. It is a synthetic version of the natural hormone that our body makes to balance blood-sugar levels."

He expertly shook the vial until the powder was

completely dissolved, then refilled the syringe with the liquid once it became clear.

"Does anyone know how old she is?"

Lina asked the crowd and received mixed responses.

"Somewhere between sixty and seventy. She is a *babcia*—a grandmother—here on a visit, they think."

"Good. And I'd guess she's around eighty-five kilos," he continued, almost to himself, as he filled the syringe with most of the liquid. "The good thing about this stuff is you can't put in too much. But if we can be as accurate as possible..." He stopped in midflow to flick the syringe a couple of times, squirt a tiny bit out and raise the woman's skirt until her upper leg was visible. "Hold her steady now." Holding the needle at a ninety-degree angle, he injected the contents into the outer edge of her thigh muscle. He sat back on his heels, pulling the woman's skirt back down over her knees as he did so, and watched as her jerky movements slowed.

"Would you two be all right helping me roll her into the recovery position? Just follow my lead." Cole looked between Lina and the young man who had helped her. They nodded and gently helped him turn her on her side, where someone else laid a knitted blanket over the woman's side.

As they waited, Lina could hear the group discuss the situation. Would Irina or Marja's blanket be softest? Should they get one of the pillows Mrs. Wojek had cross-stitched for the new settee? What about the ice cream? Who had made the ice cream that day and why had no one noticed this poor woman sitting on her own fainting like that, and, my goodness, who was the handsome doctor? He looked like a television star sweeping in like that from the dance floor.

Lina felt a smile tease at her lips, only trusting herself to keep her eyes on Cole's fingers as they tracked the woman's pulse.

After what felt like the most interminable wait, the woman's dark eyes flickered open.

A relieved smile lit up Cole's eyes. "Can we still get that chocolate? And maybe a meat sandwich or some crackers and cheese? There's no need to rush because the medication will make her feel nauseous for a while, but she may need something to nibble on if the ambulance gets stuck in traffic."

Lina rattled off the requests, even though she

could see people already responding to Cole's questions, and asked the woman her name. It was Beatrycze, the same as one of her aunties. She smiled up at Cole, aware he'd have no idea of the coincidence but happy about it nonetheless. His quick thinking had potentially saved this woman's life. The sound of sirens began to infiltrate the air around them, abruptly wailing to a halt.

"Looks like you beat the emergency services to it." Lina couldn't keep the pride out of her voice. She knew she hadn't had anything to do with the woman's recovery—it had all been Cole—but she felt proud by proxy.

"My parents will be pleased all the tuition they spent on medical school was put to use," he quipped, his face shifting seamlessly from bright to dark.

She'd seen that look before, the one that clouded over those bright blue eyes of his. Her heart ached for him. As their eyes met, it was all she could do not to reach out and touch him, hold him as he'd held her when it had all seemed too much. Not that she'd told him anything. She hadn't been ready to talk about the hurt that had virtually shredded her heart into worn threads. Seeing him now, like this, she knew she would be safe confiding in him. He had hurt as much as she had. She was not alone.

"Looks like someone's been busy. Whose handiwork is this?" A man in a paramedic uniform appeared with another man close behind, carrying a large first-aid kit.

Cole rose and rattled through what he'd done and what he suspected the situation to be.

"We'll take her to hospital and they can run through some tests."

"No." Beatrycze pushed herself up to a sitting position. "Please, no. I prefer to go to Polskie Centrum Zdrowia."

"This isn't a taxi service, love. It's an ambulance. We go to St. Andrew's Hospital or the Royal. Your choice."

Beatrycze turned to Lina, visibly distressed, and began speaking in Polish. "Please, I am new here—only visiting. I know the Polskie Centrum Zdrowia. I don't know enough English to go to the hospital. I am fine. I will just go to my son's." She tried pushing herself up to standing, but wobbled halfway up, was caught and steadied by the sea of hands lurching forward to help her back to the ground.

"She doesn't have to come with us if she doesn't want to," interjected the paramedic. "We can't force anyone to come with us. But if she was my nan I'd get her somewhere to be checked out."

"I think it might be best if you go see a doctor," Lina said to Beatrycze in Polish, then continued in English, her eyes trained on Cole. "Perhaps you will let me accompany you to the Polskie Centrum Zdrowia, if that would help."

He nodded with a smile. "Sounds like a good idea. Want me to come?"

Igor barked from the bench and Cole shot his gaze back and forth between the two of them. "You'll be all right on your own?"

Beatryzce gave Lina's hand a grateful squeeze. It was the first time in a long time Lina had been the one who'd been able to help. The wash of thankfulness it gave her surprised her.

"Yes." She nodded her confirmation to Cole, too full of emotion to trust her voice not to shake. "Yes, we'll be fine."

CHAPTER SIX

"YOUR USUAL?"

"Yes, please!" Cole realized he was using his "bright" voice. The one that tried to convey happiness when he wasn't feeling it naturally.

"You and your wife must love our ribs. You buy so many!"

"Oh, there's no wife." Cole felt himself go on the defensive. He always bought enough so he'd have leftovers. That was sensible, right? Or just something that a bachelor would do to avoid the "cooking for one" scenario he loathed.

"Why don't you have a wife?" The Chinese woman who always took his order wore an expression of pure mystification. "You're not ugly." She rocked back on her heels to study him. "You must have a good job to buy all these ribs…"

"Uh…yes. I'm a doctor." He hoped he didn't look as gormless as he felt.

"Then what's wrong with you?"

"Just busy with work, I guess."

"Then you work too hard. It's not smart to not have a wife. There's no balance. No harmony." She shook her head decisively, then disappeared into the back where he heard the rapid-fire cadence of Mandarin fill the kitchen.

Cole scrunched his shoulders up, then jigged them up and down a few times in a stab at relaxing the line of tension tightening his shoulders. He scanned the Chinese restaurant that, as far as he was concerned, made the most delicious ribs in the city. Not to mention some ridiculously divine garlic beans. And the place was never empty. He took in the couples murmuring quietly over plates of dumplings, greens, noodles. Children delighting in the turntables at the center of their family tables, sharing not just the great food but conversation, smiles, laughter.

He looked down at Igor, sitting obediently by his foot. "Guess it's just you and me, buddy. Eh? No danger of exchanging garlicky kisses with anyone tonight."

Igor's floppy ear perked up to meet the other as Cole knelt to give him a scratch. It went straight to Cole's heart every time Igor's ears collided at the top of his head. "So much for you going back to the shelter..." Igor opened his eyes wide, then leaped at Cole for a few slobbery licks. He couldn't help but laugh. A couple of months ago he wouldn't have dreamed of getting a dog, let alone hanging on to a goofy mutt abandoned by his moonstruck receptionist.

Where was she now? he wondered. Dancing beneath the Spanish skies? Dancing...like he and Lina had been.

Good grief.

Talk about moonstruck. If he didn't watch it, he knew he'd be as moonstruck as Scarlet and there was one strawberry blond, rose-lipped reason why. He had come so close to kissing Lina tonight. Ice-cream cones and visits to the Polish Centre, where a whole new side to her had come to light, were going to have to be stricken off the list if he was going to retain any sort of professionalism between them. He'd take it up as a mantra if necessary: theirs was strictly a working relationship. Work, work, work, work, work and...not even a bit of play?

All right, fine. His day improved from the moment he lit eyes on her and went downhill before they'd even finished saying goodbye. Truthfully? He knew he was stage-managing as much time with her as he could. It would've been easy as pie to sort out different classes for Igor, but knowing he'd see Lina again after a full day's work took the edge off the growing emptiness of his self-imposed hermit-like life. But there was a reason he was alone—had to be alone. Not monk-like. He'd definitely dated women since Katie had had her car crash—but commit to one? Take on the responsibilities he'd had with Katie? Bear the weight of her family's grief and his own? Their pain? Their fury at the unfairness of life?

"No more dancing from here on out. It's going to be just us menfolk, Igor."

The puppy's brow furrowed in consternation.

Fair enough.

"Guess we'll both take some convincing, won't we, buddy?"

"Double order of ribs for *one*."

Cole took the takeaway bag, trying his best not to acknowledge the restaurateur's pointed look. Fine. Enough already. He was an unbalanced, off-key bachelor. When you'd made the set of bad decisions he had, that's what happened—and on days like this you just had to learn to suck it up.

"It isn't protocol."

"It *is* common sense." Lina stood her ground. Or, more accurately, kept her seat beside Bea—as the woman was now insisting she call her. "If she wants me to be in the room with her, then you should let me. Isn't the patient always right?"

"I think you mean the customer."

"This is a private clinic, isn't it? Bea will be paying you the same money as everyone else."

The women looked at each other and nodded in tandem.

The doctor gave Lina a pained expression. She felt for him. He was just doing his job, but so was she. Well. It wasn't really her job, but Bea needed someone to look after her. To help. And for the first time in a long time she was feeling properly...*useful*. "At least let me stay through the examination until her family arrive. We rang them on the way here."

The doctor's eyes darted between the pair of women before nodding his assent and proceeding with the examination. Lina could barely suppress the happy smile forming on her lips, then decided to just go for it. Why not? She was happy.

Sure, she felt helpful at the clinic, answering the phones, doing the files, greeting the patients and so forth—but here, helping Bea explain what had happened at the Polish Centre, detail what treatment Cole had given her, she felt like she was actually making a difference. More than just commiserating with a dancer over a bad landing or a *relevée* gone wrong.

Later, when Beatrycze's family came, overwhelming her with thanks and gratitude and a small bottle of cherry slivovitz, it really was impossible to keep the smile off her face. As she pushed the door open to leave the clinic, the doctor who had been treating Beatrycze approached her.

"Miss Keminsky?" Lina turned to him. "I'm glad I caught you."

"Did I leave something behind?" She did the obligatory pat of handbag and pockets to make sure she had everything she'd arrived with.

"I just wanted to say thank you."

"For what?" Now she was mystified. She'd done

little more than sit with Bea—well, *insist* she sit with Bea.

"We normally don't get NHS translators coming along with the patient. Obviously, we speak Polish here, but it was useful having someone who'd been with her from the beginning of her situation. Usually, you lot are too busy to take the extra step."

Quizzical lines formed on her brow. "I don't work for the national health."

"Oh!" He looked surprised. "I just presumed. You seemed to have a good understanding of everything that had happened so I thought you were a medical translator. If that's not what you do, you should consider it. My understanding is that they always need people. Any other languages?"

"German and French." Lina answered on autopilot, and then quickly backtracked. "My German is a bit rusty."

"Well, if you want a career change I would check it out. It's always great for the patients when they know there's someone fighting for them."

Work as a translator? The idea had never occurred to her before but as she waved goodbye to the doctor and let the idea settle in…translator…

the spring to her step grew a little bit lighter. She was halfway down the street before she realized she was heading in the wrong direction to get home. She had automatically aimed for the underground station that would take her to the clinic. Her intention had been clear. To share her news with Cole.

It hit her like a thunderbolt. She was falling in love with him—which was mad! She hadn't even kissed him yet. Not that that was part of the falling in love To-Do Checklist, but... But nothing. There were about a million things they hadn't done yet but even so, her heart squeezed tight, then burst into an interior fireworks display. She was falling in love with Cole!

She wanted him to know everything, hear everything, be her North Star, hold her when she was happy, sad, exhilarated, scared and...oh! Just everything. Not that they knew the slightest thing about each other.

That wasn't strictly true, either. Lina forced herself to focus. Cole knew a lot about her but she knew remarkably little about him. Was it enough? He was kind, smart, funny, made her a little weak-kneed. Well, very weak-kneed—particularly whenever he unleashed that slow-motion wink of his. He did seem to enjoy spending time with her—or was that just guilt because of how much she helped with Igor?

Or was it all in her head?

The questions whirled and whirled to the point she could almost feel herself spinning along with them. She squeezed her eyes tight to make the world solid again. Real. It all boiled down to one thing—was she worth falling in love with? If she didn't even feel she could face her parents, she could hardly be worthy of someone's love.

She stopped in front of a shop window and took a good long hard look at her reflection. This was serious. Life-changing. She saw her reflection's narrowed eyes. This was tough—and necessary. It was time to start asking questions. The hard ones.

Was it worth sacrificing a chance at genuine happiness and love to fall back into the familiar vortex of insecurity Cole had pulled her out of? Or had she reached a point in her recovery where she finally had it in her to fight?

She'd done something really good today. Something rewarding. And the doctor at the clinic had noticed. Perhaps if this was a new niche she could explore for herself, a new purpose…something that would help her rebuild a sense of worth… maybe then she could let herself begin to believe that whatever it was that was happening between Cole and her could be real. She crossed her fingers and gave a quick look up to the heavens for good measure.

Please, let it be real.

"Someone looks busy. What have we got here?"

"Oh, it's nothing." Lina swept the papers she'd been reading into a pile.

"That's not a job application, is it?" The displeasure in Cole's tone was unmistakable.

"No, of course not." Her mouth went dry and she felt a chill shoot along her spine. The guilty kind. She could hardly compromise the job she had for one she could never get.

Lina hurriedly stuffed all the paperwork she'd been going through into a drawer. "Just something I was doing for Gemma." She looked up and met Cole's gaze, her breath catching in her throat as it did nearly every time she permitted herself to enjoy the azure clarity of his eyes. Uh-oh. Was this what he looked like when his hackles were…?

"She's not getting you to do her work for you, is she? I'll have a word."

"No! No. Please, don't. It's fine." Lina hastily covered with a plastered-on smile. What a mess! Served her right for telling a white lie in the first place. Biting back the fact she'd been looking for medical interpreter jobs, she handed over a wodge of messages.

"You've got a tendinopathy case next and after that a spondylolytic back injury and two posterior decompensations of the torso. Both teenagers."

"Get you!"

"What?" Lina looked at him blankly.

"You and all your medical lingo. *Shebam!* You've settled right in."

Please don't look so impressed.

"Nothing I didn't hear in the rehearsal halls my whole life. Plus I like saying spondylolytic." Lina smirked, trying to look lighthearted without belittling the condition. A fracture to the back was no laughing matter. Neither was her predicament. She might know these things, but from the research she'd just done it wasn't enough to just magically become a medical translator.

On top of which, she didn't want to add to Cole's

stresses. He'd been working crazy hours lately. Dancers across the capital seemed to be tearing tendons, axing their Achilles and destroying their knees like it was going out of style. Good for clinic business, but the light shadows under Cole's eyes betrayed the fatigue he must be feeling. His work was his life and this week it was easy to see the wear and tear that sort of commitment brought on. She longed to reach out and give his hand a comforting squeeze but holding back came more naturally.

Especially now.

An internal groan wouldn't hurt anyone, so she let one unfurl across her rib cage, then felt it land with a weighted *thunk* in her belly.

Why, oh, why was life so full of obstacles? Where she'd felt so hopeful and excited for the past few days, just daring to believe she might have found a new calling in life—*urgh!* The leaded weight of disappointment sat heavily in her belly, the familiar feelings of failure building up like storm clouds in her psyche.

She'd scoured the sites of five recruitment agencies online and speaking Polish and English wasn't nearly enough. Many of the posts preferred it if you were actually a medical professional as well as being bi- or trilingual. University in the UK was no longer free, not to mention the fact she was about a hundred years older than any of the other students would be—

"Hey, there." Cole's broke through the roar of thoughts drowning out any and all confidence she had gained lately. "Everything all right?"

"Of course. I am just thinking."

"Thinking pretty hard from the looks of things." Cole picked up another handful of messages she'd put in his cubbyhole and sifted through them whilst giving her a periodic glance as if she would suddenly open up and spill the beans.

Why couldn't she? Why couldn't she just tell him everything?

Because, you first-class fool, it's unprofessional. At least one of you should remember he's the boss.

"It's Igor, isn't it?" Cole's face was the picture of gravity.

"What is? Nothing's wrong with him, is there?"

"We-ell…" Cole teased out the word with agonizing slowness. Despite herself, Lina's hands clasped together over her racing heart. She couldn't bear anything to happen to Igor. "He's been missing you." Cole gave her a pointed look. "Have you been feeling the same way?"

The breath she'd been holding whooshed out of her chest. Was Cole giving her an out? A way to avoid talking about what was really troubling her? Her heart sunk.

Wait a minute. Maybe it was the other way round and— Wait another minute! Did she actually *want* to tell him?

That was new.

Baring her very soul wasn't really her style.

She looked up, almost surprised to see he was still there, patient as ever, an expectant smile playing on his full and far too kissable lips. Her heart shot back up into her throat. Maybe… No… She chanced another glance. Was Cole offering her an excuse to spend time with him? Making it possible for her to open up? Show him her heart?

She swirled a finger round an invisible dust heart on her desk. "I do miss seeing his little furry face around here. It's not the same without him."

"It seemed sensible to send him to puppy day care instead of keeping him in my office. Socialize him," Cole explained, long fingers scrubbing at his jawline as he spoke. His eyes went up to the ceiling and on a long journey around the reception area as he spoke again. "Maybe you'd like to come to dinner with the two of us?"

Lina didn't answer right away. Of course she would, but with the knock to her confidence she'd just had she wasn't so sure it was a good idea.

"I know a great place that has outside tables and killer catfish. Good old-fashioned American soul food." Cole's eyebrows did a little jig. "Remember? I said I'd have to pay you back for making me eat beetroot ice cream the other day."

"Hey." Lina swatted away his insult, laughing at the memory of the face he'd pulled. "I didn't *make* you do anything."

"Lina Keminsky, let me make this very clear. I don't think there's anyone in the world who could've coerced me into trying that purple swirly whatever it was apart from you." The air turned electric as their laughter shifted into a taut silence. Was he thinking of the moment he'd held her in his arms while dancing, looking into each other's eyes, when it would've have been so easy to go up onto tiptoe and kiss him? So perfectly easy. Her lips parted. She couldn't help it. Her entire body ached to be closer to him. Was this the risk she was meant to take? Being with Cole?

"Is that a yes?" He looked as transfixed as she felt. Lina only just managed a nod. Her entire insides had turned to jelly. It'd be a miracle if she managed to get out of her chair and walk anywhere, let alone to dinner.

"Any messages, Lina?" Gemma's cheerful voice cut through the thick atmosphere.

"Oh, yes, sorry. There are a couple." Lina shook her head, almost convinced Cole had hypnotized her into saying yes.

"Gemma," Cole interjected, his tone taking a decided swing into boss territory. "You're not getting Lina to do all your paperwork, are you?"

Gemma shot Lina a questioning look and received a rigorous *deny, deny, deny* micro-head-shake in return.

"Yup—sorry. My bad!" Gemma chirped, giving Cole a smart salute. "Won't happen again, boss."

Cole looked between the pair of them and shook his head. *Women!* his face said. He grabbed a sticky note, scribbled something on it and stuck it to Lina's computer screen out of Gemma's sight as a woman with a neck brace came in the front door.

"Right. That's me back to work." He gave the girls a quick nod and, with a practiced smile, began to steer his patient toward an exam room.

"Ooh!" Gemma crowed. "Someone's in trouble!"

Cheeks burning, Lina pulled the sticky note off her computer and held it in her lap.

Eight p.m.—Uncle Sam's in Borough Market

Warm swirls of anticipation began to fog her mind.

"What were you doing anyway?"

Lina started and stared at Gemma.

Apart from staring at Cole and wishing I was kissing him?

"Nothing."

"Yeah. And I'm a talking tiger. C'mon, Lina, I've seen the looks you two have been exchanging. Someone looks like they've got a crush on the boss!"

Heat crawled up from Lina's neck onto her cheeks as Gemma's singsong teasing rang through Reception. Had she been that obvious?

"Not that I blame you," Gemma continued, oblivious to her mortification. "Cole's hot. No getting away from that. If you're the one who can crack that veneer of charm and get to the amazing guy we all think is underneath there, more power to you!"

"I don't think—"

"Lina." Gemma leaned on the reception counter and gave her a studied look. "There is nothing wrong with fancying someone. I'm just saying be realistic. The guy is…" Gemma paused, choosing her words carefully.

What? What is the guy? Gorgeous? Charming? Kinder than anyone she'd ever met before?

Out of her league?

"The guy seems to be a keeper. In my book anyway," she qualified.

"Have you dated him?"

"Oh, blimey—no way. Not my type."

Lina couldn't stop her eyes from widening. As far as she was concerned, Cole was like a Hollywood star—someone with a mass appeal factor.

Gemma laughed good-naturedly. "For my sins, I love me a bit of Viking. Shaggy blond hair, blue eyes, big huge arms that look like they could wield a sword or throw a log at marauding somebody-or-others…"

Her gaze drifted off into the middle distance for a moment, clearly besotted with an invisible Viking in their midst before shaking herself back into action. She grinned then paused. "What was it you were trying to pass off as my work anyway?"

Lina gave a quick scan of the corridors leading to the exam rooms. No sign of Cole.

"It's nothing really, I was just looking at some jobs."

"What? You've not even been here three months yet. Are you not enjoying it?"

"No, no. It's nothing like that. It's just—"

"Just that you're a dancer who can't dance anymore and you're trying to find your place in the world?"

Lina's jaw dropped. Few people were that blunt with her. "Uh—something like that. Yes."

"Look. I was in the same shoes as you a few years ago. Remember your first day? You've got a much better chair, though! It took a lot of work and a lot of soul-searching, but when I kept finding myself following the patients into the physical therapy rooms to set them up for their appointments and then not leaving…well…" She gave a happy shrug. "I guess I found my place! If you've found something like that, go for it!"

"I don't think it's as easy as that."

"Nonsense. Nothing is harder than becoming a professional ballerina and you've already ticked that off your list. Tick!" Gemma made a huge mark in the air with a flourish of her hand. "I'm going to take a wild stab in the dark and imagine you've got self-discipline in spades. I took all the energy I used to pour into rehearsals into my training. I have zero doubt you can do the same. *Zero*," she added for good measure. "What you did at the ballet was amazing. How many dancers get to be a prima ballerina? And you've got to move on at some point, right?"

Lina managed a half shrug. Maybe? Yes? Could she really ever let it go?

Gemma's finger did a quick rat-a-tat-tat on the counter. "The fact that you're even here proves you've done the hard bit in moving on."

Lina's forehead went into crinkle mode. "What do you mean?"

"In comparison to the life of a dancer, *everything* is easy..." Gemma headed toward the staff room, then turned to give Lina a mischievous wink and giggle. "As easy as falling in love!"

Color flooded Lina's cheeks again as Gemma giggled her way out of Reception. Was it that easy? Just letting go of the years and years of intense rehearsals and classes and sacrifice? Heaven knew the release she felt when she'd wept in Cole's arms all those weeks ago had felt like mourning of sorts. As if she'd been saying goodbye. And now here she was, looking for a job she never would have dreamed of doing before. Maybe it was all just part of her journey through life, a bit less "one direction" than she'd thought but...

She looked down at the note she was still clutching in her lap and smiled.

There was hope there—and possibility. All she had to do was believe in herself. Believe if she set her mind to it she could get a job as a medical interpreter. Believe that Cole was asking her out on a real, honest-to-goodness date. Not out of pity but because she was worth it. Even if it was just for a night. Her fingers drummed along the phone console. A sudden urge to call her parents took hold of her. She tapped out the numbers before she could talk herself out of it. The ringtone sounded and she struggled against a gut instinct to hang up again, as she'd done so many times before. She could do this. Her parents had loved her before she'd been a ballerina, and now she had news—lots of it. She worked at an amazing clinic, she'd helped a woman she'd met at the Polish Centre and despite her very best intentions she was falling head over heels—

"Słucham."

Lina couldn't stop the tears springing to her eyes at the sound of her mother's voice. It had been too long.

"Mamo, to ja. It's me, Mama." The words washed through her again and again as her mother laughed with sheer delight, then whooped and shouted for Lina's father to pick up the other line.

For the first time in years Lina believed her own words were finally true. *It's me. Lina.* Not Lina the dancer, the receptionist, the dog walker, the failure. She was none of those things and all of them at once and there was one man who had been key to helping her get to this point. She traced the words on Cole's note as she chatted with her parents. Would she be enough to meet his expectations whatever they might be?

From the happiness in her parents' voices, perhaps she could begin to believe "just Lina" was enough for them. And maybe, one day, they'd even have Lina the translator! The thought of how much lay ahead of her was simultaneously thrilling and daunting.

What did Cole expect or want from her? "Just Lina?" With the scars, the feet that would never look great in sandals, the steep, steep learning curve she still had to climb in life? Would she be enough?

She hoped so. With every pore in her body she hoped so.

CHAPTER SEVEN

"WHERE'S IGOR?"

"I thought he looked a bit tired—it's just me, I'm afraid."

"Oh."

Cole replayed the opening moments of their "date, not date" on a loop as he watched Lina disappear into the ladies' room. Talk about an unmitigated disaster. This was worse than he could've imagined. A cotillion filled to the brim with women of his mother's choosing would have been better than this! Seriously better. And that was saying a lot.

Lina's expression had been unreadable when he'd broken the news he was there on his own. Just a neutral expression, eyes refusing to make contact with his, the menu providing the only distraction.

Just dandy! She'd shown up to see the dog. And there was him thinking she'd agreed because she'd wanted to go out with him. Have "grown-up time" away from the dog, the clinic. This was the first date in years he'd gone out with expectation, with hope. And it was gnawing him apart. He began to rearrange all the condiments on the table to occupy his jangling nerves.

He'd never cared before what the women he'd gone out with had thought of him because he'd known he'd never tell them. Never let them know the real Cole. The guy who'd tried to please his parents by marrying the right girl and having it go about as wrong as it possible could. But Lina deserved more. Deserved to know the truth. But the truth would most likely destroy what had been growing between them, the growing flirtation… No. It was more than that. More than a flirtation. He had feelings for Lina, but with that came respect. Honesty.

Ha! Showed him. She'd probably agreed to come out tonight because he was the boss. He'd kept her late at work countless times before… For the love of Pete! Had he really misread the "ice-cream overtimes'" as romantic rather than what they most likely had been: plain old politeness? Years of practice at his parents' country club had obviously dulled his people-reading skills. Then again, he'd just presumed everyone there had been faking perfect lives. It's what everyone did. Right?

He looked up to the ceiling and offered it a silent howl. He should've just bailed there and then. *Why had he left the dog at home?*

"Could I please have some more water?" Cole signaled to the waiter. He'd already had several refills, but the glasses here were so dinky. Or were they? Was it more the case that he was feeling like the world's largest oaf and everything was out of perspective? He tried to size up his water glass. Properly. Objectively. Like he normally sized things up. Scientifically.

Hmm. Okay, *fine.* It wasn't really that small.

He was nervous, all right? He hadn't been out on a proper date in who knew how long. Not that this was a date. Lina had clearly met up with him to see Igor. Igor, the blameless, adorable, lovable puppy.

Talk about showing up with your heart on your sleeve. Maybe his parents had been right. He'd never learn to truly play his cards close to his chest.

He folded and refolded the napkin, glancing toward the ladies' room as if she'd swoop right back out of it, all smiles and adoration.

He struck what he hoped looked like a relaxed position. He'd been tense all evening. As had she. He readjusted his pose. It wasn't as though he'd never been out with other women before—obviously! But usually it was a group thing, or— *Nah. Nope. C'mon, man! Quit with the excuses.* The truth was he was falling for Lina hook, line and sinker, and this so-called date was a first-class disaster. It wasn't going to work when he told her what she was getting into, who she was really with. A rudderless, banished doctor who had single-handedly torn the heart out of his hometown.

He scowled at the largely untouched plates.

Blackened catfish and cornbread weren't Lina's things. Not that she'd said as much—she was too kind for outright criticism—but the food on her plate hadn't been eaten, just rearranged, and as for the conversation? It had hardly been sparkling. He should've backed off and headed for the hills after the hush-puppy starters.

Maybe he should just be honest. Tell her everything. The first day they'd met his intentions had not been altogether altruistic. Madame Tibold had caught him at a weak moment. He had just been lumbered with a puppy, lost his receptionist and everything had just seemed to fall into place to give a girl down in the dumps a helping hand, which, in turn, would help a guy who was down in the dumps.

And then she had turned out to be…Lina.

It was hard to even think her name without superimposing it onto his psyche in huge glowing letters. He hadn't meant to fall for her. Seriously. He hadn't. Not now when so much was still up in the air in his own life. He let his head fall into his hands.

What would she think when she found out he'd pulled the plug on his own fiancée? They'd only just become engaged. The only saving grace was that no one knew his feelings for Katie hadn't been as strong as hers had been for him.

Not that it mattered in the long run. After her parents, his parents, and the community had effectively written him off he'd survived by convincing himself he didn't care what anyone else thought. But this time he cared what happened. Really, really cared. And it scared the daylights out of him. He wanted—no, he needed—Lina to know what she was getting into and the idea that the truth could send her running—

"Was I gone so long that you fell asleep?"

"What? No—not at all!" Cole half rose from his bench seat as Lina rejoined him in the booth.

"Sorry."

"Sorry." They spoke simultaneously, laughed, looked away and then looked back, eyes caught with each other's, and— *Ah!* There it was again. That electric connection he had convinced himself he'd fabricated. There was nothing imaginary about it now. It sizzled between them, alive with expectation. The only question that remained was what to do with it.

"Do you want to get out of here?"

"Yes."

Thank you, Eastern European directness. Lina rarely minced words and he liked that.

He signaled to the waiter for the check.

"Shall I take you home?"

He knew the words were in total opposition to what he wanted, but this was up to Lina...choosing him.

She shook her head. The movement was so small at first he thought he'd imagined it. When he saw her lips begin to curl up into a smile, a hint of pink warming up her cheeks, Cole felt a surge of energy charge through him—something more powerful than he'd ever felt before. He wanted Lina. Had done from the moment he'd laid eyes on her. She deserved to know the truth about him. How and when he would tell her about the real Cole was yet to be decided—but he would tell her. Right now? Something more primal was at work. Something he couldn't ignore.

Cole quickly paid the bill and was up, helping Lina into her jacket, before either of them had a chance to reconsider. Was that a shiver of anticipation he detected in her? He slipped a protective arm across her shoulders. He would be careful with her. Gentle. Loving. He may have a past, but so did everyone—and not all of it was bad. Tonight it would just be the two of them, present in the here and now.

Just a guy on a date with a girl.

Lina could hardly keep a single thought straight as she and Cole made their way through the twists and turns that made up Borough Market until they reached the Thames. She'd been so nervous the entire date she was sure the only thing on Cole's mind had been how to get rid of her. Had their stilted conversation simply been because he was feeling the same way—jittery with anticipation? Riddled with nerves that they would be enough?

When they emerged on the broad esplanade they stopped for a moment as if neither of them had ever seen London before.

The riverside view was absolutely beautiful. Everything seemed crisper tonight. More...*real*. The air positively hummed with life. Tower Bridge, all lit up, fountains awash with light, street food vendors hawking delectables from every corner of the globe, and couples, just like them, strolling along the riverside, taking photos, holding hands...kissing. It was then that Lina realized she'd been tracing her lips with her fingers, first one then two taking a leisurely, slow slide across her lips.

Lina wondered if any of the other women felt the heated intensity of anticipation warming them from the inside out. They all looked so confident—so relaxed!

Did any of them feel the slightest teasing of fear—like she did—that she wouldn't be enough? That once Cole was with her, really saw her—

the scars, the lack of experience, the long road of recovery she still had to traverse—would the disappointment in losing him be worth just one starlit night of kisses? Had that vital moment of connection they'd had in the restaurant been as real for Cole as it had been for her?

Insecurity threatened to overwhelm everything good about this moment—the "right nowness" being with Cole always seemed to elicit.

It would be so easy to just run away. Run back into her flat and curl into her well-worn nook of the beaten-up sofa, hiding away from the world, her fears. Easier to live with her own personal disillusionment than adding Cole's disappointment in her to the pile. But maybe…could they just have this one night? One night to see if what kept setting her body alight with desire was real?

She looked up at him and received a warm smile in return, a little squeeze on her shoulder and a nod out toward the river where a boat was going past, the deck filled with well-dressed revelers toasting a bride and groom.

Wait a minute. Was Cole showing her his intentions? No. That would be madness. Then again…

Running back to the flat suddenly didn't seem

such a great idea after all. What was it her grand-mother had always said to her when she'd dropped her off at her dance lessons as a little girl?

Serce nie kłamie. The heart sees further than the head.

The saying didn't extend to include a forecast as to how accurate the heart's vision was, but who cared? The very atmosphere of the spring evening was magical and, as if the Queen herself had just announced a decree, Lina knew it was time she stopped letting niggling doubts destroy the mood. She let herself snuggle a bit closer under the comforting weight of Cole's arm, peeped up at him and smiled. How could she not? She was a different person from the one he'd coerced out into the world.

Imagine that! A different person in just under three months. Or maybe she was simply allowing herself to become the woman she'd been all along?

"C'mere, I want to show you something." Cole slipped his arm off her shoulders, his fingers wrapping through hers with a little tug to run up the steps of Tower Bridge with him.

She pushed any reactions to the twinges she was feeling in her hip to the side. No pain, no gain—

right? And just about everything that had led to this night was gain.

Her focus was so complete on matching his stride, feeling her fingers woven through his, the smile that might never leave her lips, she'd hardly noticed they had arrived at the center of the iconic bridge, festooned with lights and offering one of London's loveliest river views. Cole turned her toward the view and stood behind her, his hands shifting along her elbows until he'd folded his arms and hers into a cozy twist of limbs and hands. His and hers. She closed her eyes against the view for a moment and just let herself be completely and wholly absorbed by the sensations coming to her. She let her weight shift back into her heels so that her back met his chest—his body met hers.

For the first time in months she felt *feminine*. As each moment luxuriously unfolded, Lina became more and more aware of her own body in relation—in connection—to Cole's. Her back touching his chest elicited a warming in her breasts, a tightening she could feel against the lace of her bra. His arms, wrapped loosely around her, just grazed the sides of them and she nearly moaned with anticipation of more. The crowds around them seemed to thin—or perhaps it was just the awareness of Cole that made everything else fade to a luxurious blur... She tipped her head to the side, her cheek rubbing against the linen of his jacket, the scent of him making the world more complete. As if it were a dance they'd rehearsed in another time and place and had come back to as a longed-for memory, she slipped her hand out of the weave of arms and hands and softly, slowly caressed the side of his face as he lowered his lips to kiss her cheek.

Lina's body came alive in a way she had only ever felt onstage, but better. Nothing in the world mattered now but Cole. His touches, his caresses. Who was she kidding? All of it! Being in his arms, smelling him, feeling her fingers pressing into his arms, his lips moving along her cheek to her jawline, each microsecond was the fulfillment of a dream she'd hardly let herself believe could come true.

As if by design she turned and was instantly caught up in a tight embrace, their lips meeting in a searing synchronicity of movement, touch and exploration. How could something be so sweet and suggestive at the same time? A silent giggle tickled through her midriff when she realized she was actually weak-kneed. Thankfulness for the strength in Cole's arms flooded her as he held her close.

Kissing Cole, touching him, being held—upright!—by him felt like precious discoveries. A whole new world of hidden treasures. Joyful treasures she would let herself enjoy for tonight. She opened a far-off hidden door in the recesses of her mind and pushed and shoved all her insecurities inside and locked them away. Hadn't they earned a night together without her past weighing her down?

As Cole's kisses deepened, she felt the warmth in her heart begin to billow and flood her entire bloodstream. Through some unspoken message only their bodies knew, they simultaneously broke away from the slow, exploratory kisses—the feeling and intentions too intimate to carry on anymore in public.

Forehead to forehead, their breath intermingled as Lina traced her fingertips along the sides of Cole's face, delighting in the topography of his cheekbones, the spackle of shadow bringing further definition to his jawline, that sexy little gap between his teeth visible now that her finger had traced his lips into a smile. She chanced a look into his eyes and was relieved to see the same swirl of questions and answers, all of them bearing the bright sheen of expectation.

The silence that shrouded them as Cole took her hand and waved for a taxi was unsurprisingly taut with anticipation. The only words spoken on the short journey to his place was the address, as if saying anything more would break the spell.

Cole didn't trust himself to speak. The only words he could think of were meant for Lina's ears only—not those of the taxi driver, who appeared to be disappointed no chitchat was forthcoming. He had to smile. What a change to have some good news to share with someone in lieu of the usual exchanges over disappointing weather or snarled traffic. He pulled Lina in closer to him, pressing a light kiss onto her forehead as her hand slipped onto his thigh. He put his hand over hers and held it in place, far too aware of how his body would react if she were to shift her fingers toward the inner length of his leg. He was already feeling heated pulses of response below his belt, his tapping foot a sign of his growing need to be inside his house, the door closed solidly behind them so that they could explore this entirely new world they were creating. A Lina-and-Cole-centered world where even the lightest of kisses elicited volcanic surges of response.

The taxi driver was paid, and Cole held the front door open for Lina, hoping he would be distraction enough from his haphazard stab at decorating. Her eyes widened with delight as she dropped to her knees. *Interesting.* He didn't think the new wallpaper was that amazing.

"Igor!"

Ah. Of course.

Rather than let "puppy time" break the mood, Cole leaned against the corridor wall and smiled at the pair's happy reunion. It struck him how they'd both come into his life on the same day— each having an unexpected impact. A good one. Having the two of them in his house—everyone just enjoying *being*—made the place feel more like a home than it ever had.

"What do you say I pour us a glass of wine and we can take Igor out to the garden for a little run round?"

Lina's eyes shone with happiness as she pressed herself up from the floor. "You have a garden?"

He was on the brink of saying "of course," before remembering she only had a tiny flat and a dramatically different income. Another reminder to be more aware of all he *did* have in his life rather than what he didn't. Focusing on the empty holes in his life had been a bit of a forte these past few years. Maybe it was time to start letting all of that go. What he had—right here and now—was very good.

"Wow! It's beautiful." Lina's whispered response to the sight of his garden brought Cole an unexpected swell of pride. It certainly wasn't any near as big as the garden he'd had back in Carolina, but for London it was a good size. Buckling down to pay off his medical-school bills straight away had made this possible. A slate patio stretched out from the back of the house, the handful of pots he'd managed to fill earlier in the spring now coming to life with young flowers. A small lawn spread out beyond the patio steps, easy enough to mow in five minutes, big enough to play catch with his pooch. A handful of fruit trees ringed the garden. The former tenant had left him some of the previous year's apple crop. On a particularly homesick day, he'd fixed a variation on his grand-mother's apple cobbler—a bachelor's variation—and had eaten the whole thing in lieu of supper.

Igor romped out onto the grass, throwing Cole a look, and it was difficult not to interpret as one of gratitude. The pup hadn't been a huge help in getting the garden up to scratch, but his arrival had compelled Cole to work on it a bit more. In-vest some time and energy on filling the empty flower pots, mulching the trees for the first time since he'd arrived a year earlier.

He stood at the kitchen window, opening the bottle of wine as he watched the pair of them. Funny how everything he'd wanted to rid him-self of—attachments, responsibilities—now held the promise of possibility. Of family. He didn't want to be Lina's boss tonight. He wanted more. Much more than might be possible, but watching the two of them—Igor receiving a huge cuddle before Lina pushed herself back up to enjoy the garden again—he was going to let himself believe for tonight. Believe in possibility.

Igor embarked on an exploratory trip, weav-ing in and out of the bushes and shrubs lining the garden fence, Cole and Lina no longer of interest to him. He had the neighbor's cat to sniff out, and city foxes to guard against. Cole set the glasses of wine on the patio table, not the least bit interested in whether it was a premium vintage or some mass-market plonk. He pulled Lina into his arms, keen to pick up where they'd pulled themselves to an unwelcome halt on the bridge.

Using a single finger, he swept first one then another thick coil of her honey-red hair behind her shoulders. Now that she was in his arms again, time was no longer a factor. The only thing he would make sure of was that he made the absolute best use of it.

Lina's breath caught in her throat as Cole's index finger skimmed along her hairline. She felt her head tip and move in harmony with his movements, her eyes completely engaged in absorbing each detail of his face as if trying to imprint it on her mind's eye.

He was so beautiful. Not a word she'd usually use for someone as divinely male as Cole was—but there simply wasn't a better word to describe him. Just his cornflower-blue eyes alone were enough to enchant a woman. She'd certainly fallen under their spell. She blinked, reopening her eyes in time to see him slowly lowering his face toward hers, lips parted in anticipation of meeting her own. The surge of emotion she felt joined forces with an overwhelming rush of physical desire. Before she could let another thought enter her head she was tasting him, kissing him, hands on his chest, then around his shoulders as she felt his hands shift from her waist up along her spine, before lightly tracing along the nape of her neck. The urge to become as one with him threatened to engulf her and for the briefest of moments she went completely still. Once she unleashed her full desire for him, she would no longer be able to hide anything from Cole. She loved him and after this? She would be his entirely.

What, for the smallest moment, seemed terrifying, shifted into the most natural decision she had ever made. Cole's every kiss spoke of an identical yearning. As their kisses deepened, Lina gave in to her body's need for him. Thoughts barely took shape as her hands continued their restless exploration of Cole's body. Her fingers slipped through gaps in his shirt. Buttons came undone, breath came more heavily. Her clothes—summer thin—suddenly felt too great a barrier between them.

"Be with me," Cole whispered in her ear, hand at the small of her back as she turned toward the patio doors, fairly certain she'd do just about anything for or with him if it was whispered in that soft Southern accent of his. Her eyes instinctively shot to the garden.

"Igor's fine," he added, reading her mind. How she even had a thought for the dog was beyond her as Cole's touch took over any common sense she might have left. They ran, tripped, crawled and laughed their way up the carpeted stairs, making it only as far as the landing where Cole slowly, luxuriously pinned her to the floor, his movements as graceful as a mountain lion's, his intentions as powerful. Her hands already pressed into the carpet, Lina moaned as her hips were pressed to the floor beneath Cole's, the slow sway and pressure of his movements sending shock waves of heat to her very core. She closed her eyes as her body arched into his, his fingers teasing away the buttons of her blouse. A whimper slipped between her lips as Cole shifted the fabric away from first her rib cage, then her breasts. His fingers traced along the lace of her bra, her small breasts pressing toward his hands as they glanced across her nipples. She hadn't known the ache of desire to ever feel as all-consuming as it did now.

"Please," she all but pleaded with him. "Please, let me be yours."

Time passed in a heated blur as clothes were dispensed of and skin finally touched skin. Their intentions united, Lina completely gave in to her longing for him.

Legs tangled together, fingers sought purchase, their lips met again and again to kiss deeply, urgently, as though this were both the first and last time they would ever be together. It was a thought she couldn't bear and as quickly as it had come into her mind she banished it, taking on instead the waves of desire she was experiencing as Cole rested the entire length of his unclothed body atop hers, taking most of his weight in his powerful arms and shoulders. She couldn't help but think it was as if she had been made for this very moment. The very pressure of him unlocked an even deeper hunger for more. She could hardly bear not having him inside her. Only then, when their bodies would move as one, when they shifted and pressed and cried out together, would she feel anything nearing satisfaction. Cole rolled them both over, swiftly lifting Lina up.

In a handful of steps they were in his bedroom, a ragged moan of need filling the room as he laid her on his bed, intensely aware that Lina was virtually aching with anticipation.

"Are you sure?" Cole asked, already raking through his bedside table drawer for protection. He knew this was a game-changer. It would shift their relationship forever and for the first time in years he knew he had to take that risk.

Nodding was all she was capable of. Lina wanted Cole more than anything on earth. It surprised her to realize the thought didn't frighten her. Being with him wasn't playing on her insecurities the way she had thought it might. His hands on her body, his lips exploring and tasting her only made her feel stronger, more capable. More *real*.

Cole joined her on the bed, his caresses shifting from slow to urgent in sync with her response to his touch. When his lips touched first one nipple, then the other, Lina barely held back the cries of pleasure lying in constant wait in her throat. His fingers sought her hip bones, gently shifting along the soft curves and dips leading to her belly. As his hand slipped between her legs she was no longer able to stay silent.

"Now! Please, now!" She didn't care if it sounded like begging. Having Cole inside her was the only thing Lina wanted, the only thing that would satiate the longing she felt for him—and with a torturously slow descent he met her needs. Their movements took on the urgent syncopation of primal desire. Their bodies moved in union, each of them realizing the all-consuming ecstasy of the other's touch.

When at last their breathing slowed and steadied, Cole untangled himself, only to pull Lina securely into his arms, a finger occasionally swooping along the dip toward her waist, then along her hip before his hand came to a rest.

Lina felt sleep coming, as it was for Cole. His breathing slowed then deepened, playing softly upon the nape of her neck, and just as her eyes were about to close for the final time that night she first heard then saw a little canine figure standing in the doorway, tail wagging in a final confirmation that all was well that night in London, and—for now at least—nothing else mattered other than the simple fact that they were all together.

CHAPTER EIGHT

SUNLIGHT WAS THE first thing Cole was aware of. It played across his face with the gentle undulations of the curtain. He fuzzily remembered leaving the window open the night before. He pushed his feet into the beginnings of a full-bodied stretch— *The night before!* When Lina and he had— His hand moved to the other side of the bed. She wasn't there. Cole's eyes snapped open, his whole body on high alert.

Where was Lina?

He scanned the room as if it would offer him some answers, ear tipping upward so any auditory clues could more easily slip in. No Lina and no puppy. The house sounded deserted. Ah—maybe she'd taken Igor out for a morning walk.

"Lina?"

His call met with no response.

He was up and out of bed in an instant. Tugging on a T-shirt and a pair of boxers, he skidded down the stairs to the kitchen. A tour of the garden revealed nothing. A buzz started in his ears. Thoughts clashed against each other, drowning out logic. He'd made a mistake by bringing her here. Had he misread the situation? Had taking away the invisible boss-employee barrier pushed her away? Had she somehow found out about his past?

A little tap at the door made him come to. Impatiently, he pulled it open. Where on earth was—

"Lina!" A wash of guilty relief flooded him. His secret was safe, but the door to his heart, he now knew, was well and truly open to exposure.

"Sorry, sorry." She held up a paper sack from a nearby bakery, Igor's lead complete with dog in the other hand. "I was going to surprise you and then surprised myself by remembering that neither of us have keys."

"C'mere, you." Cole took the bag and Igor's lead off her hands, his main goal to pull her into his arms. Close. Too close. "I thought you'd gone and left me, too."

"Too?" Lina looked up at him, green eyes gone wide with curiosity.

"Oh, man." Cole gave Lina a kiss on the forehead, released her and scratched a hand across his head, buying himself time to answer. "I just... It's a long story and one I don't want to ruin our day with."

Lina wasn't so lovestruck she was willing to play the fool. Cole's distress had been plain as day. "So I'm free to blub like a baby in front of you, but you have to be Mr. Big Man and keep all the secrets of your life in your big head?"

Despite himself, Cole laughed, tipping his head toward the kitchen. "Is that one of your wise Polish sayings?"

"No." Lina laughed along, because she couldn't help it. Cole always unleashed the giggler in her. But he had stoked the fires of her curiosity. He had looked absolutely stricken when he'd opened the door.

Who else had left him? Whoever it was had made a big impact on his life.

"It's not exactly as if you've told me your life story, either, is it, Lina?" She heard the words coming from behind her and was relieved he couldn't see her face. He'd just served up a big, juicy touché.

Tell him absolutely everything?

She might be better, but being that open with someone wasn't how you survived. Was it time for a change?

"Hey." She swiveled, hands on hips and gave him a cheeky grin. "I don't suppose you have any *polski kawi*?"

The emotion-thick air relaxed a bit. They'd both dodged the truth bullet. For now.

"You want good coffee?" Cole accepted the challenge. "I will make you some good coffee! It might not be Polish but—just you wait!"

"Oh, yeah?" Lina looked dubious, even though she could already tell it would be great. From everything she'd seen, Cole didn't do so-so on anything. He poured his whole heart into things. She widened her eyes as he grinned at her. Would his whole heart be with her?

"Go put the kettle on and let the master work."

Hmm…hard to tell from that one.

"Wait, no." He laid a hand on her arm to stop her in mid-kettle-approach. "I have a better idea." He gave her a wink. The kind that sent her stomach on a whirly run of flashy-blinky carnival lights.

She pulled out a chair from the kitchen table

and, after a whimper or two from Igor, relented to a cuddle on her lap. Not that it was a hardship. Cutest puppy in the world in the kitchen with the cutest guy in the world? This was a day she'd just have to enjoy. Put a lock on the door of the room of insecurities and just enjoy.

"I hope whatever you've got in that bag has the stamina to stand up to my coffee magic." Cole spoke over his shoulder, cupboard doors opening and closing with such speed she wondered if he was planning on making a four-course meal along with it.

"It's from the *boulangerie* down the road. You know—Chez Robert?"

"Ah! Very good! Pastries, I hope? You didn't go down the health-food route?"

"I don't really think the *boulangerie* is famed for its lettuce-leaf croissant."

Lina's droll tone brought a smile to Cole's lips. He didn't even need to see her face to know it would be one of raised eyebrows and rosy-red lips pressed forward in…not a pout exactly. What was it she did with those lips of hers? It was great, whatever it was.

"Fair enough."

"Chocolate, almond and plain croissants. Two of each. You must have done something to me overnight. I only had eyes for carbs." Cole's grin deepened as he spooned richly scented coffee grounds into the small sieve of his Italian coffee pot and deftly screwed the top into place, gas burner already on high. Must be nice for her, he thought, to be able to let go of the strict diet of an athlete, because that's what the dancers were—incredibly fine-tuned athletes—and splurge on some buttery carbs.

Pulling a bottle of water from the refrigerator, Cole grabbed two glasses and turned his full attention to Lina. He'd been a bit jangly since she'd been back and needed to stop, just for a moment, and *be* with her.

"Just in case you also need to rehydrate." He handed her a full glass of water, condensation already damping up the sides of the glass.

Lina didn't say anything, but a light flush of color appeared on her cheeks. She took a sip, traced a squiggle or two along the edge of the glass, absorbed in her own thoughts.

"What do you say you be a tour guide today?"

"Tour guide?" Lina's green eyes met his, fore-head crinkled.

"Yeah. I've lived in London over a year now and I still haven't seen most of the sights. Big Ben, the crown jewels, changing of the guard. Maybe you could show me around and we'll have a picnic in the park with Igor after. What do you think?"

"Oh, I'm afraid you've asked the wrong girl." She moved her toe in little arcs from parquet square to parquet square.

"Why's that? You've lived here for years!"

"Yes, but—" She stopped, lower teeth taking ahold of her upper lip, her concentration focused on tweaking the fur on Igor's forehead into a just-so quiff.

"What? You haven't been locked in a closet the whole time you've been here, have you?"

"No, but I was locked in a rehearsal room." She wished she hadn't sounded so defensive. But there it was. She'd said it. So much for the Cole-and-Lina bubble of perfection. She let her lip scrape out past her teeth. He might as well know what he was getting into—at least a little. Before the accident, before Cole, she hadn't had much of a life—any life—outside the ballet. He had done and seen so much more than she had and beyond the world of dance she was well out of her depth.

The high-pitched screech of the coffeepot gave them both a start. Her shoulders lowered, relieved Cole's attention wasn't solidly on her, watching the tendrils of the past trying to take hold of her, pull her out of the lovely, lovely place she was in when she was with him.

On a bare-bones level, her salary had never run to those things. Jewels and palaces were for moneyed tourists or comfortably-off doctors. Not scrimping and scraping ballerinas who would be better off fine-tuning arabesques. Cole wasn't naive but he certainly didn't have a clue about her reality.

Her *passport* knew more of the world than she did. Paris, London, Sydney, New York? Rehearsal rooms were the same everywhere. Some a little warmer, some a little colder—it didn't matter as long as they were constantly perfecting, constantly sloughing away any of the rough edges, constantly on point. *En pointe.* Something she'd never be again and, no matter how hard she tried, it felt as though it would always hurt.

"Here you go. This should bring you back to the land of the living." Cole slid a mug of deliciously scented coffee and milk across the table toward her.

Lina shot him a sheepish smile of thanks, grateful he couldn't see the temper tantrum she'd been having in her head. She still wasn't there yet, in the place where she could let everything go, but for this moment, this day she would try.

"What do you say we both take in the sights of London, then? Let someone else do the work?"

"My paycheck might not stretch that far." She winced as the words came out. She hadn't meant them to be accusatory.

"I know." Cole took her words in stride. "I hear your boss is a tight-ass. What do you say you let me treat you? Me. The man you were naked with all of last night." His lips turned into a naughty smile as his eyebrows performed a hopeful set of press-ups. "Just a couple of tourists out in the big city? Wouldn't it be fun?"

She knew her smile was saying yes, but...but nothing! *Just say yes!*

"What do you have in mind?"

"Ever been on the red-bus tour?"

* * *

The sounds filtered in and out of reach. Cole pressed his ear to the wall again, where the guide had assured him he'd hear Lina standing on the other side of St Paul's whispering gallery. He thought he'd heard her, but there were so many other voices, whispering sweet nothings—*Hello... Hello-o... Hello-o-o-o-o-o*—all weaving through the beautiful tones of evensong rising from the church's choir below.

Had they been alone, Cole knew exactly what he would whisper. Hell! He knew what he would shout! *You're the most amazing woman I know, Lina Keminsky. Let's do this thing—whatever it is.* But they were words he couldn't trust himself to say despite the morning's near-confessional. He was wrong to have moved their relationship—such as it was—to this level, but his gut was working overtime on overriding his head and, last night, it had won. Every bit of him *wanted* to be with Lina. The only trouble was he just couldn't. Not for her sake. Not if he really wanted her to find true happiness.

"Are you hungry?"

The words came loud and clear in the voice he

would recognize at one hundred paces. The dome echoed with his responding laugh.

"Always."

There was a pause as their eyes caught—some forty meters apart—but the effect was as strong as if she were next to him. Closer. Being held in his arms.

Cole could still hear an intermingling of voices and messages coming from across the gallery they'd tromped up over two hundred steps to reach. He noticed Lina occasionally stopping to rub her hip, but there was no evidence of a limp and, from where he stood, there on the opposite side of the dome, she looked nothing short of heaven-sent. Rays of sunlight filtered through the iconic dome, turning her hair from gold to flax to flames and back again. They'd popped by her flat after breakfast so she could change, and the simple sage-green wraparound dress she'd chosen... *Ay, caramba!* Any man would've struggled to keep his sanity. The sooner he could get her alone and start to tease away the fabric... Whispering at long distance didn't cut it anymore.

Eyes locked with hers, Cole quickly left the throng of tourists between them in his wake. The sooner he was holding her the better. No words were exchanged when he reached her. Just an understanding. Cole folded his arms around her, tourist map dangling from one hand, the other shifting along the small of her back. He felt her hands join together in a loose clasp around his waist and he all but sighed with gratitude when she let her cheek rest on his chest. They stood like that, just listening—the whispers, the music, the hushed footfalls wending their way around them. With Lina in his arms, Cole felt the world become complete again and it scared him.

What could he offer her? More running? Incomplete answers whenever she wanted to know about his past? None of it sat right and he knew he was going to have to be honest. He'd tell her everything. He would. And if she left? Well, it wouldn't be the first time.

He ran his thumb along her arm and felt a spray of goose pimples form despite the early summer warmth. He tipped up her chin and when their lips met?

Perfection.

No awkward bumping of noses, mismatched cadences or ill-judged approaches. Just one of those slow, beautiful, film kisses where—at the very end—each pair of lips is reluctant to part from the other. He wanted more. So much more. In the interest of keeping a very tenuous grip, Cole gave her a light kiss on her freckly forehead, and felt her head come to a rest on his chest again. And that was good, too.

For today? Today they were just Lina and Cole—two wide-eyed tourists in London Town. He grinned as his chin nestled among Lina's billow of hair. If only his main attraction wasn't the one he held in his arms, playing the role of tourist would be much easier.

"Do you want to get out of here?"

"Yes."

Thank you, Lina!

"This is much better, isn't it?"

"Only about a thousand million times!" Lina's eyes twinkled, her attention divided between a short-range game of catch with Igor and long, luxurious kisses with Cole as he plumbed his memory banks for the best way to start a barbecue. Each time he pulled Lina in for another proper make-out session he sent out a silent thank-you to the previous owners, who had put up high fences. Perhaps theirs had been a fledgling romance, as well.

"Not that a day of culture isn't worth its weight in gold."

"We've already had a day of my culture," Lina riposted as she sent the multicolored ball rolling across the lawn. "Now we will have a day of yours." She checked herself as Cole's expression was an instant reminder of their disaster at the American restaurant the night before. A disaster that had turned into something a little closer to heavenly. "*Another* day of yours." She waved at the glut of groceries they'd hauled home. Turned out kissing and shopping made for an incongruous set of ingredients.

"I wouldn't say this was anything my mother would've whipped up but—"

Lina crossed to him, a glass of wine outstretched in her hand.

"What would your mother have made for her little boy?" Her face was wreathed in smiles, her tone cajoling, warm…and it took everything in his power to hide the flinch that usually accompanied mention of his mother. He turned to the shiny, unused barbecue and shook in a few more briquettes. Sure, it looked like an Everest of coals but heat was important—right?

"What's wrong?"

"Nothing, I was just distracted."

"Didn't your mother cook for you?" Her tone was still light but he could hear a new twist of concern woven through it.

"Yes, of course she did!" *Oh, for the love of some sanity!* He hated the sound of his artificial happy voice. "Go on. You tell me yours and I'll tell you mine." He raised his glass for a quick chink and a peck in return for one of her full-beam smiles.

"Moja matka..." She drew the words out so slowly he could almost see the images of her childhood table flash before her eyes. "My mother was—*is*," she corrected herself, "a very good cook."

"And what did you eat when you were a little girl?"

"Ah. Well. As a little girl I was not even a tiny bit fussy. *Borscht*, buttery noodles, *gołąbki*—they are cabbage rolls with pork or mutton—vegetables, always. I would eat everything." She tipped her head back and laughed at a private memory. "You would always find me waiting at the table, fork and knife in hand, before my father had even arrived home from work—but I learned to wait very, very quietly."

"Why?"

Lina settled into one of the wooden chairs with the demeanor of an old woman, her voice mimicking the same. It was easy to see the performer in her. "*'Głodne brzuchy nie mają uszu,'* my grandmother would say again and again. 'Hungry bellies have no ears.' Of course she was talking about the leaner days when there was no food, during the Wars and lean days—these ears couldn't hear there wasn't any food. In my case, though, it was because I was a chatterbox."

Cole burst out laughing. "You? I would say you were the least likely candidate for a chatterbox I've ever met."

Lina pushed her lips out into a rose-colored moue and shook her head. "People change. I changed early."

History began to cloud the laughter in her eyes and Cole hated to see it go. "Go on," he prodded, enjoying that her accent thickened when she spoke of home. "We were talking about food."

"Yes, well, my grandmother said it was rude to interrupt someone's focus when they were cooking with unnecessary chatter. Then, of course, my mother said it too—but a bit more…hmm, how do you say…? *Child-friendly.*" She smirked, then switched voices. "In order to know when a dish was finished you must listen very carefully. It will tell you when it is done. The fish, for example— the Polish love fish. For the fish to taste good she must swim three times—in water, in butter and in wine. When the fish has had enough wine, it will sigh and then you will know it is done."

"I guess that's in line with what my father used to say about his grilled steak."

"What did he say?" Lina scooched to the edge of her seat expectantly, happy to have the spotlight removed from her.

"He said unless it was still mooing he didn't want to have anything to do with it."

"Then why did he bother cooking it and just eat steak tartare instead?"

"Raw beef? No, ma'am!" Cole tilted an imaginary cowboy hat at her and put on his strongest drawl. "A Southerner does not eat that sort of stuff from over there in Europe. A true Southerner eats honest-to-goodness barbecue. Then again—saying that—*true* Southern barbecue takes at least twelve hours, if not twenty-four, to cook."

"Like what you're making now?" Lina eyed the selection of chicken and vegetable skewers they'd bought, ready for the grill. "You plan to take twelve hours to cook this?"

"Let's just say you're not the only one who has changed." Cole turned back to the grill and made a stab at rearranging the coals now that they'd finally started glowing a bit. His father had lectured him on evening out the coals more times than he could remember. His father had lectured him about a lot of things. *Shake it off, man.* Maybe it was one of the plus sides of not seeing the parents anymore. No more lectures.

He cleared his throat and threw a question over his shoulder, in need of a distraction from the thorny trip down memory lane. "Now, apart from eating fish very quietly, I still don't have a good picture of you as a child. Any more nuggets you care to share?"

Lina looked at Cole's back, shoulders hunched

after the talk of his father, and suddenly knew it was the same for him as it was for her. Complicated. Painful. Maybe it was the same for everyone—just the way things were when people's lives were intertwined. They became knotty and seemingly impossible to make right again.

A simple start. A couple fell in love, then life ensued and the twists and turns began—no family truly becoming the picture-perfect presentations everyone imagined others' lives to be. At the very least, Cole would surely miss his parents, being so far away. Like she missed hers.

"Pierogi!" Her voice was louder than she'd intended, but what the heck. Her mother's *pierogi* were worth a shout. Delicious little potato clouds with hidden treasures buried within their soft, fluffy—

Cole's face looked blank.

"You don't know *pierogi*? Oh…you are really missing something. Especially my mother's." Lina's legs floated up to the chair and she gave them a hug. "Everyone." She spoke seriously now. "*Everyone* brags about their mother's *pierogi*, but *my* mother's are actually, truly, the best in…definitely in the village I come from, if not the whole of Poland. She doesn't just make one type. No. She cooks with what is fresh. Just like you!" Lina pointed at the huge bundle of asparagus they'd picked up from the farmers' market on their giddy, kissing-break-filled journey back to Cole's place.

Cole had started smiling early in her narrative and didn't stop now. "You haven't tasted my cooking yet. I don't think it's quite time to put me on a par with your mother."

"Oh, when you taste my mother's *pierogi*…" Lina was off now, somewhere else. Poland, he guessed.

"Is she coming over?"

"No."

"You going home?"

"No."

Lina rose, silently gathering together the prosciutto, asparagus and a wooden cutting board before returning to the table and taking what looked to be an introspective sip of her wine.

"I have not seen my parents since my accident."

Cole already knew this from Madame, but stayed silent. She was finally ready to talk and he was all ears.

"When I learned I could no longer dance…" She

stopped to pull a long strip of prosciutto from the butcher paper and painstakingly laid it out on the cutting board to receive some asparagus. As she began to roll, she gathered emotional momentum and began again. "When I learned I could no longer dance I felt so ashamed I could barely look at myself in the mirror. In fact, for a long time I don't think I even bothered. What was the point? All I would see if I looked at my reflection was the world's biggest failure." She waved away Cole's protest to the contrary. "No. For me—my whole life—*my* life was my family's life. My mother and father did everything for me." Another piece of asparagus disappeared into a nearly transparent slice of ham. "Everything was done in our house so Michalina could become a world-famous dancer. My father's work, my mother's meals…" She cocked an eyebrow at Cole. "*Pierogi* is not on the menu for a dancer. So she took extra jobs to afford the classes, the shoes. Oh, my goodness the *shoes*! I can't even think how many pairs I might have been through. Hundreds. At least."

She fastidiously stayed on task, but kept talking as if stopping would mean stopping forever and this was the time she needed to tell her story.

"Their whole lives were my life and I worked so hard to make all my dreams come true for them— to make all the effort have been for something. And then…a bit of loose cartilage, a poorly executed plié and—poof—away it all went, down the drain or the gutter or wherever dreams go when they no longer hold you up."

"But you showed them you were made of stronger stuff than intangible dreams."

"Ah—you are partly right. Partly wrong. My dreams did come true and I could finally relax and be happy that everything my parents had sacrificed had been worth it. I saved a little money so they have that. But I wasn't anywhere near being able to properly repay them for all they did for me."

"I don't think parents really expect that."

She presented Cole with a small pyramid of identically wrapped asparagus spears and shook her head until her smile was bright again. "Well. The girl I was—am—wanted to pay them back. And then, one day, this girl met a handsome doctor."

"Oh, he was handsome, was he?"

Cole drew her into his arms, his interest in the

asparagus less important than taking a deep inhalation of Lina's summery, warm skin.

"Very."

"And what did he do?"

"He said get off your butt and do some work!" She poked him on the bottom for good measure.

Cole pressed his hips toward hers. "I'll bet you any amount of money he did not say that."

Lina giggled now, the weight of her story no longer pinning her to the ground as it had.

"He was very nice actually."

"Oh?"

"Yes, he offered me a job, which came with a puppy!"

"A puppy? Sounds like a strange man, offering a woman a puppy on the first day he meets her."

"Maybe he thinks they are both broken, perhaps they will see something in the other and get better. Or maybe the doctor is a mad scientist who can't help fixing broken things," she finished with a laugh.

"No." Cole gave her a quick kiss on the forehead and held her at arm's length. "I don't do that. I give advice, options. It's up to the person who hears it if they want to take it or not."

Lina's brow crinkled. His tone had been sharper than he'd intended. It was his sore spot and he hadn't responded well. But how could she understand what he had gone through? Effectively killing your fiancée…the one the whole town had wanted you to marry… Sure, it had been Katie's wish…well, part of one of her law classes: write your own will… They'd actually laughed at the time, neither of them having the slightest clue the price would be so dear.

Hadn't losing Katie been enough pain without both his and her families shutting him out?

Little creases appeared at the sides of Lina's eyes. As quickly as his hackles had risen, they went down again. It wasn't her fault he came with baggage. It was no one's fault. It was just life. And it was up to him to decide if he was going to drag it along after him the rest of his days, the people around him taking the unwitting fallout. Lina was important to him. He was as close to sure as a man could be that he loved her. He would have to try harder, more actively, to lay his demons to rest—or let her go.

He couldn't do that. Not yet.

He felt a sigh make him sag again. The thought

of losing Lina was one too many for what was supposed to be a carefree afternoon. He took the well-practiced route of trash-compacting his past, choosing instead to soak up a nice drink of Lina. Her beauty knocked him for six, and her soul? Still waters were running much deeper than he'd thought.

"Hey, take a look at that broken puppy now!" He nodded toward Igor, who was happily throwing a stick for himself on the small patch of lawn. "I think you probably did more to fix him than I did."

"I had motivation," Lina countered.

"And what was that?"

"Ice cream." She smiled coquettishly and blew him a kiss as she skipped down the steps to join Igor on the lawn.

Yes. He smiled back. Ice cream did work wonders. Not to mention the positive affects of some seriously memorable—ahem—nighttime activities. He surprised himself by hoping there would be more of them. Being with Lina was about the most natural thing he'd ever experienced. But they each had rivers to cross. When and if they did, he hoped to heaven they ended up together.

CHAPTER NINE

"RIGHT, TILLY! HOW are the knees today?" Cole gave the teen an encouraging smile. She was painfully shy and, according to her mother, dancing was the only thing that brought her out of her shell. A diagnosis of rheumatoid arthritis was exactly what she didn't need.

"They're okay. They hurt a bit," she replied, immediately contradicting herself.

"Let's see you walk round the office, shall we?" Cole swiftly began pushing aside chairs to make more room for her. He was walking on sunshine today and had to work hard to adjust his mood to match each of his patients. Waking up with Lina in his arms made the world a better place. But this was the workplace and he was her boss. Nice reality check. Not.

"I've been eating more fish and have totally given up burgers, which has just about ruined any social life I had left." Tilly play-moaned as she walked, with obvious discomfort, round the room. She was used to the routine. This was a been-there-done-that procedure for her and Cole felt for her.

"The changes in your diet could definitely help. Your mother tells me your kitchen is well stocked up with olive oil these days. How's your stomach dealing with the glucocorticoids? Any nausea, muscle weakness, mood swings?"

"No," she snapped. That answered that, then.

"How's your blood pressure? You were just in with the nurse, right?"

"All right," she bit out, eyes fastidiously locked on the path she'd chosen to navigate round his office.

"Does all right really mean 'not so good'? C'mon, Tilly," he cajoled. "Talk to me. We can always give you an inhaler—or organize injections, if you'd prefer."

"I'd prefer to be at ballet class with the rest of my friends!" Tilly's voice cracked and Cole's heart went out to her. Ballet was most likely not on the cards for her anymore. Quite a few things were off her list of "normal girl" activities. Instead of giggling about boys with her friends or practicing her *pas de deux*, she was shuttled between appointments with him, a physio, a dietician, a pharmacist and a podiatrist, just to name just a few of the medical professionals she was required to see simply to keep the pain under control.

"I know, Tilly."

"How could you?" The teenager wheeled round on him. "How could you understand what it's like to know the only dream you had in life will never come true?"

Cole instinctively opened his arms wide and beckoned for her to come in for a hug. He knew it wasn't the British way, but he was an American and she was just a kid. A kid having a tough time. At the very least she deserved a hug.

He felt her shoulders begin to shake a bit as he folded his arm round her and it wasn't much of a leap to remember the day Lina had wept in his arms, tears flooding her eyes for all that she had lost.

Hugs he could give. Fulfilling dreams? Hell. What he would've given to feel his own mother's arms round him after Katie had died—or felt the familiar pat and clap to the shoulder his father had always given him when things had been tough.

He'd had none of that. Not a single act of compassion. They had all but strung him up.

He pulled a box of tissues off the desk with his free arm and gave it a little wiggle in her eye line. Tilly pulled a couple from the box and allowed herself a heartfelt sob before she blew her nose and took a bit more time to snuffle and regroup.

When her breathing had steadied, he held her out at arm's length and gave her tearstained face a smile. "You know, I've been doing some reading and there is something that is meant to help."

Her eyes brightened and the hint of a smile began to tug at her lips. "This isn't another one of your hocus-pocus American things, is it, Dr. Manning?

"A little bit." He grinned. "What do you know about swing dancing?"

"What?" She crossed her arms over her chest. "Like the cowboys do?"

"Kind of. Or, if that's not your scene, there is the Lindy Hop."

"Where the boys twirl you round nineteen-fifties style?" Tilly's smile was unabashed now.

"That's the one." Cole reached across his desk

and grabbed a prescription sheet and started to scribble.

"More medicine?" Tilly pouted, immediately wiping the smile from her face.

"Something like that." Cole tore the sheet from the pad and handed it to her with a flourish.

"Go to Lindy Hop, ballroom or tango classes until something sticks. Go out with your pals. Have a burger every now and again. Get on with your life." Tilly read out loud, her voice growing increasingly disbelieving. "That's your prescription?"

"That's my prescription." Cole nodded, vividly aware, as she left his office with a wave and a smile, that he could probably afford to follow his own advice.

"Ow-ww! Wugh!"

"Stop your wiggling!"

"Stop digging your elbow into my hip!"

Gemma began to cackle. She always did when Lina moaned. "This is peanuts compared to what you put yourself through at the ballet—so grow a spine!"

"I would if—" Lina began energetically, then

stopped herself. No more excuses. She was on a path now—a good one—and Gemma was right. "What helped you?"

"Helped me what?" Gemma dug her thumbs deep into muscles Lina was sure she'd never forget she had now that she had become the massage therapist's official "hip guinea pig."

"Move on—after dance."

Gemma's hand movements became less tactical and more intuitive as her thoughts drifted off. Lina felt a sigh of relief work its way through her chest. Her new friend was a take-no-prisoners masseuse. She didn't do light and fluffy. She put muscles through their paces. It hadn't hurt this much before. Maybe so much sex after…quite an absence hadn't been such a wise move.

A little grin crept onto her lips without even taking a moment to reconsider. No doubt about it, she was on a fast track to the land of the love struck. Not that she could spin round and sing corny songs from musicals in the office. She and Cole had dealt with the working-together issue by ignoring it. Deeply mature and nigglingly not so fulfilling.

"I would say our cases are a bit different. I had

an injury I could have recovered from—*did* recover from. And then was stupid enough to go back for more when they told me not to."

"I would have done the sa-*ame*! Ow! What are you doing with my poor glutimous maximus?"

"More like minimus. And it's *gluteus* maximus, you boob. Suck it up. Your booty is tiny, Keminsky. No pain, no gain. Didn't you do all the exercises you were given after your hip operation?"

Lina chewed on her lips in lieu of answering. *Gluteus maximus.* Latin was exactly the same Latin in Polish. She would have to revisit the anatomy coloring book she'd bought herself when she'd still been dancing. The knowledge was in there somewhere. She just had to tap into it.

"Aw—c'mon. Are you telling me all that famous ballerina discipline flew straight out the window?"

Giggling, she confessed, "The doctors were just as bossy as Madame and…" She sobered at the thoughts of the months she spent hiding away. "I'd just had enough. *Don't cross your legs… Do use ice… Don't lean forward while sitting… Do use heat… Don't try to pick up something on the floor when you are sitting or bend at the waist be-*

yond ninety degrees. My favorite was, *Don't turn your feet excessively inward or outward when you bend down*—the very thing I'd been trained to do again and again and again… *Out! Out! Wider! Out!* Pfft…" So much for her enviable turnout. Now it was the bane of her existence.

"Sounds pretty familiar." Gemma twirled her finger round and held the towel up for Lina to turn to the other side. "Bossy doctors, eh? You must be a glutton for punishment to come and work for Cole."

It was impossible to stop a flush of heat from coloring her cheeks.

"Ooh! Someone's still got it bad for Cole!"

Silence was the safest option here. So Lina chose it.

"Well, as I said, whatever that man does, he doesn't do it in-house—so I wouldn't get your hopes up. He's probably got a lady brain surgeon tucked away in his garret. Or a high-powered lawyer. Maybe a bored duchess or—"

"I get the picture." Lina hoped her dry response was enough to stop the speculation of who else might have also been sharing Cole's bed. It hadn't occurred to her for a second that she might not be the only one. The thought turned her stomach. For the past forty-eight hours she'd been quite merrily floating around on cloud nine. It was the only time in the past few months she'd let herself believe she was enough for Cole. They'd been so… *whole* together! The doubts began to tease away again. He was an amazing man. Intelligent, passionate, worldly…and what did she know about life-living? The insides of countless rehearsal studios and…erm…she could talk your ear off about tutus if that was your thing, but wasn't so sure it was Cole's.

"Don't let me put you off!" Gemma dug into Lina's good hip with the same verve as she had the other. "I always say, 'Aim high!' and you're bound to catch something on the way back down to earth."

"That's very Eastern European of you."

"No. That's the school of hard knocks talking, my friend."

"What do you mean?"

"I mean—and you probably already know this, so I don't know why I'm bothering to preach to the choir—life is tough! You can't always get you want and all that jazz. Just getting a social life together after my injury was hard enough. The other dancers in my troupe closed ranks as if my injury would infect them. Getting onto a whole new horse professionally was tear-inducing and it took ages, but it was a hundred thousand million times worth every frustrating minute."

"Better than dancing?" Lina allowed herself a glimmer of hope.

"Better for me. I can work when I like. As long as Cole's cool with it," she hastily added. "I discovered I love teaching massage as much as I love doing it, and most of all I get to help people. Don't get me wrong—dancing was amazing. It was the thing I'd thought set my soul alight—but it was a blinkered existence. Just listen to wise old me—shoot for the stars and you're bound to find something."

But "something" wasn't good enough. She felt it in her bones.

Tears pricked at Lina's eyes as reality set in. She'd been a fool to think her ridiculously perfect weekend with Cole had been anything more than a one-off. She had let a part of her heart believe otherwise and was regretting it now. It had seemed better than real—it had felt deeper than real. It had felt like…felt like kismet.

Silly girl, she chastised herself. *Away with the fairies as usual.* Had a couple of months working at a new job and meeting the most divinely kind, gorgeous and completely generous man she'd ever laid eyes on really turned her pumpkin into a carriage heading for the ball?

A lone tear snaked down her cheek and plopped onto the massage table, mercifully out of Gemma's sight. She needed to regroup. Floating on air was one thing—coming down for a landing was another. She'd already indulged in months of self-pity and a fat lot of good that had done her. Now was the time to get up and soar.

"I hope you're not looking up barbecue tips."

Lina practically jumped out of her skin, caught by surprise at the sound of Cole's low voice by her ear, his breath on her neck. It had been frantically busy all day and whenever their paths crossed at En Pointe, work was work and nothing more. But right now Cole's voice was much more after-hours than not and it sent a thrill of anticipation along her spine. Until she remembered what she'd been searching for on the internet. She grabbed the mouse and jabbed at it, frantically trying to shut down the page.

"Medical translator, eh?"

Obviously not fast enough, then.

"Oh, it's nothing."

"You seemed pretty captivated by it."

"I was just looking at it for a friend." *Who happens to look a lot like me.*

Cole did that leaning, crossed-arms, sexy thing against the wall that always made her lose focus. A stream of white lies wasn't going to help the situation. Best fess up.

"Remember when you saved Beatrycze at the Polish Centre?"

"I seem to recall you doing your part, as well," Cole brushed off his role in the incident.

"Well…this is sort of what I am looking up, but I think it's probably too much. I don't have the right background so…"

"So, what exactly are you saying? You're going to give up before you've started?"

"No, it's just…" *Sheesh…when you put it that way…* "I have a job already and this is full-time and so many of the places say a medical background is necessary."

Cole swiveled her chair round so she could no longer avoid the electric-blue gaze of his eyes. Looking into them was like looking into a truth factory. It was difficult to resist the urge to squirm. Feeling giggly and sexy was *so-o-o* much easier than laying the bare bones of your psyche on the line.

"You have a job you could quit."

His words felt like an icicle in her heart. He didn't want her here any more?

"No, I'm happy. This was just silly—something the doctor at the Polish clinic said. I was just daydreaming. Besides…" she put on her best employee face "…I haven't even finished my three-month trial. It would be a show of disrespect to my boss if I were to leave so soon."

Yes. She was testing the waters, but she had to. Didn't she?

"I think your boss would want you to be happy. And if that meant leaving En Pointe, he'd cope with it."

Oh.

"Go." She twisted her chair back round to face

the reception area and flicked her fingers at him. She couldn't look into those eyes she loved so much anymore. Not without crying. "Shoo. Go away, bossman. You have a patient coming."

Cole glanced at his watch and the patient printout on Lina's desk.

"Yes, but not for a few moments." He felt the crease on his forehead take up position. It always settled in the dead center of his eyebrows when something weighed on him.

"Lina, you're not…?" He'd been going to ask if she was hanging around because of him but the arrogance of the suggestion made him back off. That and their "all work at work" rule. But he was the boss. He could break the rules, right? Or was he the one who needed to set an example?

"I'm not what?" There was a note of anxiety to her voice he didn't like to hear. He'd put it there and upsetting her was not on his agenda.

"You're not free for dinner tonight, are you?" *Just ask her directly, you goon.* Cole could've clunked himself on the head but opted for an expectant look.

Lina scanned the room. What was she doing?

Checking for bugs from the other practitioners? Or finding an excuse to get out of it?

"I'd like to explain a few things."

He'd meant it as a good thing, but from the set of her lips he could see he hadn't chosen optimum boyfriend phrasing.

His eyes widened at the thought. Was he a *boyfriend*? The word sounded a bit more flimsy than what he was feeling for Lina—but it would do. For now.

She tipped her chin to the side but still wouldn't meet his eyes. Was each word he was saying just another shovelful out of the hole he was digging for himself?

Maybe it would be easier if she didn't work here. All he wanted right now was to pull her into her arms and tease the color back into those lips of hers with an endless flow of kisses. His fingers flexed in anticipation of caressing her. Lordy. He had it—and bad.

"Dinner? Ice cream? A walk? None of the above?"

"Maybe not tonight."

He was going to let her off the hook and then thought better of it. No way. What the two of them had was worth pursuing—and he wasn't going to squander it away on missed opportunities. What had his dad always said? *Opportunities rarely come to you, son, so you'd better make your own.*

"Unless you've got an appointment with the Bolshoi Ballet, I won't take no for an answer."

The silence between them was deafening. Cole couldn't believe he'd just stuck his foot in it—both feet in it—in such a massive way.

"I'm sorry, Lina, that wasn't what I—"

"I know. Don't worry. I've heard you say it to the others."

Brilliant. Not even an original ultimatum. Cole dropped down into a squat and turned her chair back to him.

"Now we definitely need to talk. And not here." From the look on her face it was going to take more than a table for two to set things right.

"Fine." It wasn't her happy voice.

"We'll sort this out." He gave her a pointed look. "Tonight."

For once Lina was grateful when the rest of the day passed in a swirling daze of calls, patients, mixed-up records, updated records, appointments to change, make and cancel. A series of tiny little things all rushing together to help take away the thoughts teasing at her conscience.

Was Cole trying to end things already?

They'd had just about the best forty-eight hours ever and now it was all coming to an incredibly abrupt halt. Was he suggesting she quit? Or was she just being crazy? Paranoid? Maybe all of it meant nothing. *Everything* and nothing. Just like her. She'd had everything and now…

Jasna cholera!

Why couldn't one teeny-tiny single thing go right for her?

She knew she was being melodramatic, but right now the despair she was experiencing felt like it would eat away at everything she'd left behind. The insecurity. The physical weakness. The pain.

She had felt so incredibly alive—not just over the past few days but the past few weeks. Especially when she was in Cole's arms. Her entire world had brightened.

The welcoming reception area suddenly felt suffocating. The plants, the beautiful soft furnishings, all the things designed to put people at ease had her on edge. She needed to get up—away from her chair, the room, the clinic.

Just *out*.

Get some air—some fresh air. Oh, how she longed to let loose and run out into the fields behind her parents' house. Just run and run and run into the depths of the wildflower meadows and collapse in a sweaty heap by the river. It was a fail-safe cure-all. She pressed her fingertips into the edge of her desk and closed her eyes, forcing herself to steady her breathing. She wasn't going to let herself fall into that black hole of funk again. It was forgivable—sort of—after her accident. But now that she was back on her feet again? She'd have to see about closing ranks on her heartstrings a bit. But she could do it.

A cup of tea would have to stand in for the wildflower meadows of Poland for now.

Standing by the kettle, she closed her eyes again, slowly moving deep breaths in and out of her lungs. Ten, nine, eight…and one.

She was being foolish. Silly. Yo-yoing emotions were normal for a youngish woman in love. Right? She let the sound of the boiling water drown out her thoughts, just as she had that very first day she had walked into the clinic as the receptionist hopeful, and into Cole's life. She'd known he'd be something special from the moment she had laid eyes on him and she didn't want to let that go. Not now. Not when things had only just begun. She needed to show him she had resolve. Commitment. Tenacity. Whatever you wanted to call it. Cole had given her an opportunity—to work here at En Pointe and face her demons head on.

"Enough in the kettle for two?"

Gemma appeared at her side, mug in hand.

"Of course."

"You're the tops, Lina. What would we do without you?"

Lina poured the water for her, an ironic smile playing on her lips as Gemma left the kitchen, still dunking her herbal teabag in and out of the mug.

What indeed? She didn't have a clue if it would be the best thing or the worst thing to find out.

"I can't believe you found this place!" Lina's ear-to-ear grin was the perfect reward for ages trawling the internet to find just the right place. Chmurki—Little Clouds—was famed for its *pierogi*.

"We-ell, I don't know how close this will get you to memory lane as far as your mother's cooking will go, but…" Cole picked up his menu "…we'll give it a go, shall we?"

"There are so many amazing things…*i nie może odebrać.*"

Cole laughed. He had no idea what she'd just said, but it was nice to see Lina lost in the food of her homeland. By the third time the waiter came to see if they were ready, they had finally settled on their choices and ordered. Cole leaned back against the cushioned booth seat, grateful for the privacy it afforded. This was going to be harder than he'd thought.

"So, how are things going for you at the clinic?" By the sharp glance he received, the casual note he'd been hoping to hit hadn't worked.

"Is this my review? It's not quite three months."

"No. I just wanted to make sure you were happy in the job."

"It's great. Fine!" Her enthusiasm didn't quite reach her eyes.

"Hey, it's me you're talking to—not Dr. Manning. It's just Cole."

Her shoulders relaxed a bit, but the worry lines remained. "I am very happy at En Pointe. So grateful you gave me the chance."

"Hey," he quickly countered. "You're the one who got me out of a tight spot, remember?"

"Mmm… I'm not so sure that my spot wasn't a bit tighter than yours." The memory of the piles of unpaid bills, the cold air in the flat, the aching loneliness threatening to creep into the very marrow of her bones came to mind.

"Don't forget the help you gave me with Igor."

Lina felt her heartbeat quicken. What was this? Everything about it felt discordant. Even her skin felt clammy. Was this the Cole she had spent the weekend with? The warmhearted, laughing one who couldn't stop pulling her into his arms, nuzzling his head into the crook of her neck and whispering sweet nothings one after the other?

She couldn't help it. Her hackles rose. If he was going to break her heart he needed to speak to her like an adult, a woman. Not a broken little girl who needed a cuddle with a puppy.

"You know, I am not five years old. I used to dance until my feet bled—real blood. Real pain."

Now it was Cole's turn to look startled. "No, I know that. It wasn't my intention to—" He stopped, scrubbed a hand along his short shorn hair and turned the full beam of his eyes on her.

"Lina, I care about you. Probably a lot more than I should."

"What does that mean?"

If a heart could break into shards, she was quite sure this was what was happening to her right now. She needed this job—but she wanted Cole. Or was it the other way round?

A buzzing began in her ears and all she could do was stare as he pressed his fingers along the edges of the table until they were white with the pressure. Perhaps he thought without the heat of human blood running through them he would be better able to realign his thoughts.

Was he trying to tell her he'd overstepped the boss-employee boundary? It was just like the ballet—strictly unspoken but strictly adhered-to social rules… Date within your "class." Prima, Primo. Company, company. And she wasn't in Cole's class. That was becoming very, very clear.

"If you think I am not professional enough at work, I will improve. I can improve. This job is very important to me."

"Is it?"

"And here we have two *pierogi*—one with pork, one with vegetables." The smiley waiter slid the plates onto the table between them, either oblivious to or pretending not to notice the staring contest in progress.

"Bon appetit."

"Smacznego!" Lina grimaced a smile at him.

When the clinking of fork against plate became too much for her, Lina broke the silence. "What is it you want from me?"

Cole's gaze rose from his plate to meet Lina's after a moment's reflection. "I want you to do what you want to do."

"That's a bit loaded."

"Look, I've been making a complete mess of this by trying to beat around the bush. What I'm trying to figure out is why, after I've seen you check out those translator sites, you aren't going for it? Are you really happy at the clinic?"

"I don't know if there is a right answer to that." The few bites of dumpling she'd managed to eat sat leadenly in her tummy. She laid down her fork, giving up the charade of enjoying her meal.

"Do you want to do something else?" Cole persisted.

"I'm not in a position to do anything else." It took a lot of strength for her to admit it. Acknowledge that finances were still tight. It had, after all, only been just under three months since she had begun the job and there had been a lot of financial catch-up to do, even considering how generous the salary was. She folded her serviette, place it on the table and wove her fingers together on her lap, her posture returning to that of the days when she'd just received a rollicking good telling off from Madame. She knew how to take it on the chin.

"Can't you speak to your parents?"

"And become further indebted to them? I don't think so."

"But you have a good relationship with them, don't you? They support you."

"Is that how it is with your family? Support on tap?" The words had the desired effect and if she could have done anything to reverse what she'd said, she would have. Cole looked absolutely stricken. She'd never seen pain so vivid on a man's face before. Without another thought she was on his side of the booth, his head between her hands, forehead to forehead. "I'm so sorry. I'm so sorry. What have I said?"

Cole slid his hands up to cover hers, pulling

them down from his face and holding them to his chest. "People who love each other sure know how to hurt each other, don't they?"

Lina's eyes widened, glassy with emotion.

Wait.

Had he just told her he loved her?

"Families," he clarified, instantly regretting it. Could this conversation go any more south than it already had?

He did love her. Whole heart. Whole soul. He'd shout it to the hills if there were any! But he didn't seem to be able to tell her. *Why couldn't he just tell her he loved her?*

It was lay-the-cards-on-the-table time.

"Let's get out of here, shall we? Hampstead Heath?"

"A walk would probably be a good thing right now."

Finally. Something they were agreed on.

She surprised herself by giggling.

"What?" Cole's expression was suspect.

"Did you see the waiter? His face?"

"You mean the one who looked like he had the juiciest gossip in the world when we paid the bill after barely eating a thing?" Cole lifted a wry eyebrow.

Lina could only nod she was giggling so hard. Nerves? Most likely. Nothing about this day was what she had thought it would be and the careening emotional ride she'd been on didn't look as if it was near being over. Cole's face had already turned sober. As a counter, she could feel his fingers reaching for hers.

Had Cole just told her he loved her?

...*when two people love each other*...

"Turn left here."

The tree-lined avenue leading to the heath was a welcome visual antidote to the emotional rawness she felt. They'd touched on all her hot spots in a matter of minutes—seconds even—and it was hard to feel she'd risen to the occasion. Where had the single-minded girl she'd always been gone?

She chanced a glance at Cole. His blue eyes were doggedly focused on the path leading into the park. His grave expression was at odds with the gentle to-and-fro caresses his thumb was giving the back of her hand. Perhaps he wasn't even conscious of it. Perhaps it was his way of saying he was sorry.

She stopped herself. Cole didn't have anything to apologize for. He was the head of a clinic, her boss and her lover. Those were a lot of positions all rolled into one and if he saw that she was prevaricating—not showing commitment—all these questions were well deserved.

"Cole…" She wasn't quite brave enough to look at him as she spoke. "If this is about the job. I am there. One hundred percent I am there."

"Thank you, but it's not really about the job. Not right now. I need to tell you something. It might make it easier for you to understand what I'm about to do."

The tendrils of calm she had begun to feel evaporated instantly. She sat down rigidly on the bench he selected, away from the pathway where couples strolled, dogs were being led home after a walk or a swim in the ponds…where life was happening. They sat and watched other people's lives for a moment, Lina too frightened to say any more.

"Five years ago I was like you," Cole began. "Well, not like you—obviously I wasn't a prima ballerina but I was feeling at the top of my game. I lived in a great town, was number one son—well, the only son of a pair of ambitious parents who'd poured all their hopes and dreams into me, and then one day—" His voice caught and with it Lina felt her own lurch into her throat. He stared straight ahead. Not looking at her, not touching her. Was that what his childhood had been like? Bereft of emotion? Hers had been a walk in the park by comparison and it was painful to hear his voice flick into a virtual monotone. Survival skills, she supposed, for relaying the hardest memories. She knew the drill.

"Then one night my girlfriend—actually, she was my fiancée. I'd proposed a few weeks earlier, much to our parents' relief." Cole stopped and shook his head as if trying to get it all straight.

Lina's fingers wove together over her heart. It was already easy to tell this was going to be difficult to hear. As he continued, Lina's concerns were realized. It was painful to listen to. Heartbreaking to absorb.

"Katie, my fiancée, was the daughter of my parents' best friends. She and I always snuck off together during our parents' mandatory cocktail hours, dinner parties, picnics, country club dos... whatever. You name it and Katie and I were there. You know, playing board games, tennis...whatever. Our parents hung out together *a lot*. It was only natural—or inevitable—that we started dating."

"You said you were engaged." Lina's head shook in confusion.

"We did—we were." He gave one of those faraway laughs hinting at a time when life had been a bit more golden. "She'd known what I was going to do before I even started to bend my knee."

He looked at Lina blindly, the churn of emotions overriding anything else. It killed her to see this man—so very much in control of himself—completely at sea as he relived whatever it was he had gone through.

"Shortly after we got engaged—really soon— she asked me to sign a living will for her as part of an exercise she was doing at law school. For her, it had meant more than getting good marks. We'd had a close friend in high school whose parents had all but drowned in sorrow when their son had been injured in football practice and ended up on life support. Katie had been horrified when their grief ultimately led to an acrimonious divorce over whether or not to keep their son's life support going. It turned her into a vocal advocate of DNR if the victim had no brain activity. She insisted she never wanted me to have to go through anything like that. Not to mention the fact she couldn't bear the thought of a machine keeping her alive. So I thought nothing of it. I signed!"

He held his hands up as if being held at gunpoint. The expression on his face wasn't much different.

"We were young, invincible! Cole and Katie! Our parents had been friends forever and now we were set to be married. Just as our parents had half joked about—but not so secretly hoped for—for so many years."

Lina couldn't stop her nose from crinkling. Her childhood had involved so much choice! Again and again her mother and father had sought assurance that she was doing ballet because it was what she really loved. There had been absolutely no pressure from them. If anything, she would have bet money they wouldn't have minded an iota if their little girl had chosen a quiet life in the village where they lived. They had been happy. The three of them. It sounded nothing like the preprogrammed checklist of Cole's childhood. Her fingers curled round the edge of the wooden bench and squeezed. Hard. Hearing this story really made her miss her family.

"I know," Cole said, misinterpreting her expression. "It took me a while, but I finally stopped resisting."

"Resisting?"

"The inevitability of Katie and me getting married. And the smiles! They were so absolutely happy." Cole's face echoed his words as if reenacting a treasured moment. "I'd finally done the right thing. Their only child a doctor, their future daughter-in-law a fledgling lawyer—up and coming, but well on her way to a Supreme Court judgeship, they told everyone, voices brimming with pride. Sometimes I think they loved her more than me." He said the words without malice, but there was obviously a little boy somewhere inside the man sitting next to her still hoping for his parents' approval.

"Were you in love with her?" The words came out before Lina could stop them.

"I loved her," Cole acquiesced, scrubbing a hand across his head. "There weren't fireworks or anything. But she was a beautiful woman. Smart.

Funny. We'd been all but promised to each other since birth."

"That must've been…" Lina sought for the right word and was poleaxed. "A bit weird?"

"Yes and no." His head tipped back and forth with the words. "We'd always been great friends and dating each other came naturally. We knew each other like…like family."

The sadness in his voice was almost more than Lina could bear and it wasn't even her story. She ached for Cole and couldn't think of a single thing to say that would help.

"So what happened?"

He cleared his throat, simultaneously pushing himself back against the bench as if seeking additional support. When he began to speak she barely recognized the voice as his own. Autopilot was more like it.

"I was at work one day, late shift at the hospital, and the ER paged me. The rest followed in a daze, really. The car accident had been extreme. Katie's vehicle had slid under a jackknifed lorry and the impact had resulted in massive brain trauma. Traffic was heavy, despite the hour, and it had taken some time—too much time—for the ambulance to arrive. Her doctor was taking me through her paperwork—the DNR—when her parents arrived and begged, pleaded with me to reconsider. As if I could!" He shot Lina a glance, eyes so full of emotion she was sure he was asking for her to agree with him. She nodded along, unable to begin to imagine what she would do if put in the same place. It was obvious he had loved Katie. Maybe not passionately, but she couldn't believe Cole would've asked her to marry him just to please his parents.

"My family, her family—they all swore she was responding. But in this case it was all false hopes. She'd been brain dead before she arrived at the hospital."

He paused for a moment as a family group wobbled past on shiny new bicycles, the youngest towed along in a bright red wagon looking as though he was having the time of his life.

Lina envied them the carefree evening they were having, then checked herself. They may have known hard times, too. They were as deserving of a fun night as the next person. Or—she crossed her fingers beneath her thigh, where her hands remained trapped—the person next to her. *How*

*on earth did you give the go-ahead to end the life
of a person you loved?*

Abruptly, Cole clapped his hands together. "And
that was it for us as a family. They've not spoken
to me since."

She heard the words but found it hard to reg-
ister them. No matter how horrid she'd been to
her parents, they had made it explicitly clear they
would always, *always* be there for her.

"You mean your fiancée's family?"

"All of them. None of them." He looked her
straight in the eye. "My parents haven't spoken
to me since and with the loss of their support so
too went the faith of my patients."

Lina's fingers flew to her lips in a combination
of horror and disgust. Abandoning Cole like that
when his grief had been as heavy as theirs? How
could they have done that? He'd had to regroup
on the edge of a coin.

"Don't." He shook his head at her. "Seriously.
I get it. Intellectually, at least. My parents are a
really smart pair, and that's how they deal with
everything—clinically. It's just who they are.
They'd become so attached to the idea of what my
future had in store they just couldn't bear that the

reality didn't match up. They were grieving the loss of the woman they'd hoped would be their daughter-in-law and wanted someone, *anyone* to blame. It was impossible for them to accept that the future they'd planned for me—us—boiled down to *paperwork*."

"But it was a car accident! You didn't have anything to do with that. And she wanted the DNR!" Lina couldn't help but jump to his defense. Cole wasn't the one in the wrong here.

Cole's head fell into his hands. Elbows on knees. Back hunched against the world. Lina resisted the urge to give it a rub. Console. Caress him. Everything about him screamed injured wild animal right now—one that would lash out if touched. She knew it wouldn't be personal. It would be that the pain was too unbearable.

He sat back, scrubbing away invisible tears. "Since then I've made it a practice not to pressure people into anything. Force them into doing something they don't want to. Doctors aren't gods. People need to make their own choices in life— that's what I've preached from the moment I left Maple Cove." He turned to face her, his eyes, his face still beautiful despite the sorrow etched into them. "Which is why I regret to inform you that while your services will be required for another week, En Pointe will not be renewing your contract at the end of your three-month trial period."

"I'm sorry?"

"I'm firing you, Lina. You're fired."

CHAPTER TEN

"You're fired."

She blinked.

What?

He repeated it.

Shaking her head to make sure she'd heard him correctly, Lina looked at Cole again. His mouth was set. Hands folded together. Shoulders spread out broad, as if expecting to be challenged. His whole body was braced to defend himself.

She didn't need to hear him say it again. It was obvious what was happening here. He was finishing with her. Personally, professionally—what else was there?

Her first instinct was to protest. On a bare-bones practical level, she *needed* that job.

"You'll be given two months' pay to tide you over, as I realize this didn't come with much warning—"

"Are you *kidding* me?" Lina felt herself go into

flight-or-fight mode and in that instant her prover-
bial dukes were up. She was ready to take him on.
Or be blown away with the lightest breath of air.

Cole could have run her over with a steamroller
and it would have felt better. Why tell her everything he had only to blow her off? Was it meant
to lessen the pain? Because he'd hurt, too? She
didn't even know where she stood on that front.
Her lips parted, but nothing came out. An enor-
mous "why" hung in the air between them.

Strangely, the world stilled when she thought it
would race.

"I did it because you're afraid of being good at
something else."

"What does that mean?" He'd officially just lost
the right to pass judgment on her. "I haven't yet
had a chance to become good at the job I had up
until five seconds ago."

"Don't be ridiculous, Lina. You had that job
nailed in minutes. You're kind, intelligent. Ob-
servant. It doesn't take a genius to do it. Madame
knew you'd be fine."

"Madame? What's she got to do with it?"

"She—" He thudded his forehead with the ball
of his hand. "You weren't meant to find out. She

rang me and asked if I'd interview you for the job. I didn't want to." He stared at his hands. "I didn't think you could do it."

"Of course. What would make you think a lowly, broken ballerina could?" Lina couldn't help retorting, vividly remembering Cole's poor attempts at showing her how to work the phone system.

"Lina, please. This isn't meant to hurt you. I just think you're closing yourself off to what you really want to do because you're afraid to start over."

She stared at him, disbelief fueling the growing heat in her chest.

"The medical translator jobs?" he prompted. "You're interested in it, yes?"

"Yes, but—"

"But what? Why don't you go for it?"

"Because of the money. Because of the time. Because of the hours and hours and hours of my life it will eat up so that I will never be able to pay you back—pay back my parents. Do you want me to go on?"

"What do you mean *pay back*?"

For an intelligent man, Cole looked utterly flummoxed.

"I told you already." Lina sunk back into the bench. Bone tired wouldn't even begin to describe how she was feeling.

"Your parents? Paying things back? I thought you were over that."

"How can I get over that when I am also busy paying back debts to you? The cycle is endless—"

"You don't owe me anything!" Cole flung his hands out wide as if it would help make his point. "What I'm trying to talk to you about is moving on from that. If you see kindnesses as something that only builds up a list of debtors I—I really don't know what to say. Do you expect things from people when you are kind to them?"

"Of course not."

"Then why do you think anyone—your parents, me, especially me—would expect *payback*?"

Lina felt the prick of truth in his words but was too furious to give in.

"I thought you didn't like to make decisions for people."

"I thought you didn't like handouts." He regretted the words the moment they were out of his mouth because the truth was he was letting her go because he loved her. He loved Lina completely and believed with every pore in his body that if she stayed at En Pointe she would only grow to resent it—and then one awful day resent him. And he couldn't risk that. Right now he would live with her rage. Her anger. He'd said it before. Anger he could work with.

"Why are you punishing me for what happened to you?" Lina's voice was saturated with sorrow. It was impossible to know if he'd done the right thing.

"I had a lot of decisions made for me and I'm making just one for you. One that—believe it or not—puts us on an even playing field."

"What? By *firing me* we're now suddenly equals?"

He stopped himself from reaching out to hold her hand. She was better than him. More open. More honest. "I suppose that's up to you."

She shook her head and rose to leave, one final green-eyed look of disbelief clouding her face as she turned to go.

His gut told him to chase after her. His heart told him it was pointless.

He huffed an unhappy laugh out into the cooling night air. Maybe he should have gone after her. Explained further.

Nah. Nope.

She had a lot of information to process and interfering more than he had? Making things worse would be pretty easy about now.

He'd done the right thing. Right?

History did have a cruel way of repeating itself.

"Budge over, Manning, I need a coffee."

Cole did his best not to flinch at the volume of Gemma's voice. Turned out no sleep and a night of emotional turmoil did not a charming Cole make.

"Blimey. Did you see Lina this morning? She's all smiley and everything, but her eyes…she's not *present*, you know? Like an alien crawled into her and ate the real Lina."

That was one way of putting it.

"What? We're playing the silent game this morning and no one told me?"

"Sorry, Gemma. Just a busy day ahead. A lot on my mind."

Gemma turned to face him. Recoiling would have been too strong a word for her reaction—but he was guessing from her face he wasn't looking his best.

"Uh…boss? Everything okay?"

"Yeah, fine." Cole buried his real response behind his coffee mug before taking a much-needed gulp. Then another. "We're going to need to look for a new receptionist. Let me know if you know anyone who'd be a good contender."

He'd never seen anyone do an actual double take before. Wasn't his world just full of firsts this week?

"What about Lina?"

"I've decided not to offer her the full-time position." He drained his coffee, only just stopping himself from throwing the mug against the wall. *What a mess.* All the coffee in London wouldn't help him today.

"Any particular reason why you're not renewing the contract of one of our best receptionists, like, ever?"

"It just wasn't the right fit." Cole gave her his best this-conversation-is-over look.

"Don't you like her? I thought you two were thick as thieves!" Hands were on hips now.

Gemma went in for the kill. "She's the reason your dog is well behaved."

He grimaced in response. Yes, that was true. And Igor would no doubt run away from home now. The potential disasters were piling up. Great. His first decision to interfere in someone's life in years and what do you know? First-rate disaster.

"And the filing system is now actually comprehensible to everyone who works here."

He drummed his fingers along the countertop and raised his eyebrows expectantly. It was torture listening to the wonders-of-Lina speech when all he wanted to do was agree.

"Not to mention the fact she is absolutely gorgeous. That hair! I mean, have you ever seen anyone with hair like that? And those green, green eyes—a ridiculous shade of green! Who *looks* like that?"

His glare was entirely ineffective.

"And the patients love her." Gemma glared for added impact. *"Love. Her."*

"All right! All right. Enough. It just—" He scanned the room, searching for the right thing to say when there just really wasn't any right thing to say. "It simply isn't going to work out. Okay?"

He gave what he hoped looked like a remorseful nod and left the room. If Lina wanted to be with him she would have to believe in herself before she could believe in him. How he hoped she would get there. Gemma's voice followed him down the corridor.

"Let it be heard that I think you're utterly mad, Cole Manning!"

On that, we can agree.

Returning to En Pointe the next day was a big enough hurdle. Sitting in her chair—correction, *the* chair—right at the heart of Reception, plugging in her headset as she pasted on a smile. Each moment was pure, unadulterated torture. But she had her pride, as if that were a mercy.

Cole had been pretty clear about seeing out the final week of her trial and, painful as it was, she knew if she could do it—face the man she loved in the wake of his rejection—she would be able to endure anything. She had once danced until her feet had bled, for crying out loud! Madame had taught her that. She'd just pretend it was class and then…she'd start over.

Just the idea of it made her shoulders sag.

The situation—her impending lack of an anchor—brought an added sharpness of focus to the day. Ironically, she'd seen life through a sort of hi-def filter when she'd begun falling helplessly, hopelessly in love with Cole…this was the same but with dark edges. Cole didn't love her. Hadn't even wanted to hire her in the first place! She'd been little more than a grudging *favor*.

How could she have been such an idiot? Just seeing what she'd wanted to in lieu of the writing on the wall. Cole didn't love her.

"Alyssa Thornton, to see Dr. Manning."

A young woman stood in front of the desk, tears swimming in her eyes, crutches just visible above the high reception desk.

"Yes, of course. Let me just get your records pulled up here."

"He won't have any yet. This is a referral." The woman didn't even bother to wipe away the tears beginning to trickle down her cheeks.

"Oh, no! Let's get you some tissues. Come." Lina was up and out of her chair in an instant. She knew that pain and it was awful to see someone else going through it. "Come sit over here and I will let Dr. Manning know you are here."

"Is he a miracle worker?" The girl's dark brown eyes pleaded with her for a positive response.

"Yes." She didn't even take a moment to consider it. He might be many things she didn't like right now, but he would always be a good doctor. "He will help you. It may not be how you want to be helped, but he will help you." Lina gave the girl's shoulder a quick rub before putting her headset back on and ringing through to Cole's office. The sound of his voice did its usual magic and she fought the urge to pause and savor it, knowing this would be one of the last times she would hear it.

"Alyssa Thornton for you."

"Thanks."

And the line went dead.

She ducked her head below the reception desk, actively stemming the threat of her own tears. She hadn't been able to think straight when she'd stormed into her flat the previous night, bag thrown to one corner, jacket thrown to another, shoes unceremoniously flicked who knew where. She'd just needed to sit, as she had so many times before, and stare at the wall as if it were some sort of magnolia-colored oracle. Three months ago it had been all she'd thought she had. But it hadn't been the wall that had helped her in the end. It had been Cole.

And what had her gut instinct been just now? To defend him. To acknowledge that sometimes the best advice wasn't the advice you liked—but it was what you needed to hear.

Had that been what he was trying to say to her? "Alyssa?"

Lina swiped at her eyes before looking out into the reception area. Cole was helping the girl with her crutches, offering compliments from the get-go. "You're pretty quick on those things for a newbie!" And she may have just imagined it, but she was pretty sure he took an extra moment to look across at her—to meet her gaze—the crinkles round his eyes etching his face with more worry and concern than she thought he deserved. He deserved happiness, joy—and she'd just left him there alone, thinking only of her need to hide away and lick her wounds. Just as his family had after that awful, awful night with Katie.

It was all Lina could do to stay in her chair.

Her heart absolutely ached to be near him, with him. His pain was woven into her soul now and...

Urgh! How had everything become so complicated? Was it all really very complicated in the end? She loved him and everything he'd said to her was true. She was living her life fearfully. Worried about paying back the impossible. The only real way she could pay back her parents was to love them. To be kind. And to acknowledge in her heart that Cole didn't feel the same way she did.

She'd have to let him go.

"*Psst*, Lina—come with me."

Gemma crept up to the reception desk capering-thief style, her hand cupped to the side of her mouth.

Lina shook her head, not trusting herself to speak. Not just yet.

Gemma, never one to take no for an answer, jerked her head melodramatically toward the kitchen. "*C'mon!*" came the insistent stage whisper.

A line lit up on the telephone control system. Lina pointed at it, and gave a "sorry...can't" shrug, grateful for the reprieve. Her eyes traveled toward Cole's office as she took the call and wondered how she'd do it. How she'd ever fill the Cole-sized hole in her heart.

Eighteen cups of coffee wouldn't hurt him, would it? Not just this once…

Taking advantage of the fact no one else was in the kitchen, Cole reached for the sugar jar. He'd been counseled, when he moved to England, that when one had had a shock, a cup of tea with a spoonful of sugar did the trick. Coffee was going to have stand in for tea today.

"Oh! Sorry." Lina, lunged for the corridor, looking like a startled deer.

"No, don't go, Lina. I'm just on my way out." They did one of those awkward doorway dances where no one was going to come out the winner.

"Here, after you." He pulled the door wide open and flourished a hand for her to enter. He still wasn't sure whether making himself scarce or making himself available was the best way to go. Indecision seemed to be winning at this juncture.

"Thank you. Sorry. Thank you."

Nervous laughs filled the room but Cole didn't seem to be able to get himself to leave. There had been so much left unsaid when Lina had left the park. How deeply he felt about her, how being with her made everything better, how losing Katie had been heartbreaking but to not have had a lifetime with her hadn't been the biggest blow. He'd sat on the bench for another hour until the memory of Igor sitting alone had propelled him homeward. Home to a house that felt distinctly emptier without Lina in it.

"Cole." Her voice was a near whisper. "I just wanted to say I'm sorry."

"Sorry for what?" Cole shook his head. "You have nothing to be sorry for. I'm the one who should be saying—"

Their eyes met and the connection that had made so many moments between them ridiculously vital was back again.

"Sorry."

"Sorry."

Their voices wove together and they each laughed, Lina's fingers flying to cover up her lips as she did so. The emotion in the room was almost palpable.

"Lina! Finally!" Gemma virtually exploded into the room, not seeing Cole half-hidden behind the door. "I've been looking for you everywhere. I know it's none of my business, but I weaseled the news out of Cole that he's letting you go and I just wanted you to know how much of an idiot we all think he is. Blind!" She threw her hands up in the air as if it were the universal signal for blind and continued, hands on hips. "We all thought he was in love with you—but it shows you how much my radar is off in that department. Anyway…" she sucked in a quick breath "…I just wanted you to know how much we all value you here. How much we support you. So…I'm going to start a petition to keep you here."

Lina could feel Cole's eyes on her as she took in the rapid-fire volley of information Gemma was lobbing at her. She'd thought—no, hoped—that Cole was in love with her, too. But last night he'd told her the opposite…hadn't he? She caught a glimpse of him looking out from behind the door.

His face was impossible to read. Completely neutral. Her hopes soared, twirled round in mid-air, then abruptly plummeted back to earth. Cole had been clear. Was *being* clear. He didn't want her in his life. She should've done something she'd thought of at the beginning of the day, not skulked around. Well, no time like the present!

"Gemma, thank you so much. But please do not get any more signatures."

"Why not? You're not going to just lie down and take this nonsense, are you? Cole's gone absolutely mad!"

"No. But I must get back to my desk to write my resignation letter." She saw both of their eyes widen. "It is very nice that you want me to stay but, in fact, I think I will quit."

"What?" Cole stepped out from behind the door, much to Gemma's horror.

"Cole! Hey, didn't see you there. Sorry about the…uh…'idiot' thing. You know I love you, right?"

"'Course I do, Gemma." Cole's eyes remained locked with Lina's as he gave the frazzled physio a quick one-armed hug. "We're good."

Lina blinked. *Yup.* He was still looking at her. Blue, blue eyes swimming with questions she didn't know she had the answer to. All she knew was that she loved Cole and if launching herself at life with a renewed passion was what it took to open her heart enough to let him go, she was going to do it. Her way.

"Gemma." Cole moved into the corridor. "Will you excuse us? I think Lina and I need to have a chat."

* * *

"Comfy?"

Lina smiled at Cole's bemused expression. She'd just finished tucking her toes under her knees lotus style—her go-to position on his office couch. He was perched on the edge of his desk—not too far away—but she needed the distance.

"Very."

"Igor misses you."

"It's only been one day since I've seen him," she tutted, unable to hide the pleasure the news brought her.

"So…have you made plans already, then?" Cole skipped over the fact he was missing her, too, never mind the fact she hadn't even gone yet. But he wasn't going to push it. He'd already stuck his stick in her spokes and she'd gotten back on her bike. Just not in the direction he'd hoped.

"Yes, I would like to figure out how to go back to school. University," she quickly corrected.

He nodded, lips pressed together in a tight smile as she continued, "Learn to work with patients—translating, helping. I will be very busy. Too busy to finish my week here, I'm afraid."

A part of him enjoyed watching her give a nonchalant shrug. This was the Lina he'd fallen in love with. The one who he knew could really *own* her life. The one who shone under duress.

"We can call a temp agency to get a replacement in. No problem there. Of course," he quickly interrupted himself, "whoever they send won't be a patch on you."

"Hmm," Lina muttered noncommittally, her lips pressing into one of those lovely rose-red moues.

"I'd like to make you another offer."

"Oh?" Her eyebrows rose in anticipation.

"How about we find you a corner here, with a computer, a desk. Give you a place to start researching. I think it's the least I can do."

"No. No, thank you. I think what I would really like right now...' Now it was Cole's turn to look expectant... "Is to go home. To Poland."

"Oh." He didn't have the heart for more. His "clever plan" had backfired.

"So that I can talk to my parents. Tell them everything."

The tightening in his heart loosened. Would she be coming back?

Needing to close the space between them, Cole crossed to the sofa, took each of her hands in his, his thumbs rubbing along the backs. They were so different—he and Lina. Considering where they'd each begun life, their paths they'd started, it was a wonder they had found each other at all.

It tore his heart to let her go—but he'd made his move and the outcome hadn't been what he had hoped for. So much for Project Interference. Life was not being terribly shy about showing him his mistakes.

"Would you mind if I were to leave a few things in a corner here, in the basement? I promise they won't take up any space."

Cole snapped to attention. Oh, this was bad. "You're giving up your flat?"

"Well, I think I will probably have to if I'm going home. The rent will be money I can't afford and...well...seeing as I just quit my job I don't think my landlord will be very happy."

"Sure. Of course. Anything."

Lina tugged her hands out of his, pressing herself up and out of the sofa.

Was that it? Was she just going to leave now? Cole couldn't bear it—couldn't stop himself. He pulled her into his arms, and began to kiss her as if his very life depended on it. His hands cupped her beautiful heart-shaped face as his lips sought connection again and again with hers.

A soft cry escaped Lina's throat when Cole's arms slipped round her waist, hands shifting up her spine as he pulled her in closer to his chest.

Lina found it impossible not to respond. This would be the last time she ever felt him, tasted him. Just Cole and Lina in an office in the heart of Central London—blurring the lines of the busy day whirring past this sweet, soft bubble of perfection. She pulled back for a moment, her fingertips tracing along his face, then one by one his lips, lips teasingly trying to capture her fingers.

She didn't trust herself to brave the words aloud, making them real. *I love you.* She nodded and kissed him fervently, hoping it would be enough. Say enough. They obviously weren't meant to be and his kisses were so very bittersweet. Almost cruel.

Tears sprung to her eyes as she pulled herself out of his arms. "I must go."

Cole nodded. Said nothing to change her mind. Nothing to keep her with him.

She headed to the door without a backward glance. She was doing the right thing. When she returned home she knew she could begin to heal. It would be the first—the only—time she had seen her parents in years without having her name in lights, status, future roles for them to brag about— but she would have her head held high. When she was born she had just been Lina and they had loved her, and that was how she would return to them. A newcomer to a new way of being. Just Lina. As she closed the door to Cole's office, not daring to look behind her, she had to believe that that would be enough.

CHAPTER ELEVEN

COLE STARED AT the phone. He could feel Igor curling up beside his foot and was grateful for the support. He'd need it.

The only way he'd kept his pulse from jumping off the scale was a countless series of steadying breaths. He picked up the phone and stared at the numbers. He'd run through about a thousand different variations on how the conversation with his parents might go—how he'd even say hello—but knew the only way to find out would be to call them. It was late at night in London, but would be just after supper with his parents. They'd most likely be sitting on the porch, gabbing with some neighbors or wandering around his mother's cherished flower garden, pruning, fine-tuning, making sure it was still a contender for Maple Cove's Southern Bloom House Tours. Their house and garden, he imagined, had taken his place in their lives.

He reached down and gave Igor a scratch. The little guy had definitely pushed and prodded Cole's heart apart to accommodate a scruffy-pooch-sized place in it. It sat right next to the Lina-sized portion…a part of his heart he knew would be permanently dedicated to her, no matter what the outcome of her visit home. If that's what it was. He hadn't heard a bean since she'd left and the sheer emptiness he experienced each day without her was draining his energy stores.

He gave his shoulders a tight shrug. If he couldn't be with her, he could at least learn from her. He punched in the numbers that hadn't changed since he was a boy. The American ringtone sounded in his ear sooner than he expected and he almost hung up. Soon enough he heard the shuffle and clatter of his parents' old-time handset being picked up from the base.

"Hello?" It was his mother, her soft Southern accent shifting along the phone line straight into his soul. He'd missed her so much.

"Mama? It's Cole."

The silence that followed was as vast as the ocean that separated them.

"I'll get your father."

She put the receiver down before he could stop her—explain. Tell her how much he loved her. How broken he'd felt in the wake of Katie's death. It was so quiet it was hard to tell if she'd hung up entirely.

The sound of a second line being picked up straightened his spine. Mother and Father on the phone. Was it a sign they had forgiven him?

"Cole?"

"Hey, Dad. It's me."

"Found yourself a job?"

"Yes. Remember? I told you about it in an email. It's a specialist clinic in London. Mostly dancers."

"Oh, right!" His father's voice sounded tinny.

Cole had sent email after email at first. There had been no response to any of them. About a year ago he'd stopped trying altogether. The urge to go on the defensive had started teasing at him. The little boy in him had wanted to say, *What about me? What about my heartache? I know you lost a daughter-in-law and an idea of what the future would be—but you gave up what was real. What was living. You chose to give up your son. Your son who did the right thing, the only thing, to do in that awful, awful scenario.*

Silence lay between them. So Cole told them about the clinic, the famous dancers he had met and treated, the innovations he was hoping En Pointe would make in the future. All things that would've mysteriously found their way into the *Maple Cove Gazette* if he'd idly dropped them into conversation a few years earlier.

He could tell they were half listening, their responses lacking the energy that would indicate true interest. He couldn't really blame them. They hadn't spoken in years. He had, perhaps, been too hopeful to think they would treat his call as more than what it actually was—an unwelcome interruption to their evening.

"Mom?" There was silence. He tried again. "Mom?"

"Your mother's not up to it, son. She's not on the line anymore."

"Do you think—"

His father jumped in, his rich voice weighted with emotion, a weariness Cole had not ever heard before. "I think perhaps it's best if you just leave it, son. It'd be for the best."

"What if—"

Again he was interrupted.

"We're really pleased you're doing well over there in England. I can't keep up with the politics over there. All that shouting at each other in Parliament... Interesting. And I catch your mother checking the weather over there from time to time, so..." He let the implications drift in and settle. They cared. They just couldn't let go of the position they'd chosen that would help them deal with their grief. Their disappointments with what would never be.

"All right, then, Dad. Nice to hear your voice."

"Okay, son."

"I love you." He didn't know if his father heard the words or not, the line cut out somewhere in there.

Cole tucked a hand under Igor's tummy and pulled him up into his lap. He'd grown a lot but was still puppyish enough that he could give the furry little beast a cuddle.

He remained dry-eyed. A bit numb. The call hadn't been satisfying in any way—but if he was honest, that had been the likeliest outcome. Falling in love had cranked up his capacity for believing in change. In forgiveness.

He spun the phone handset round a few times on

the table, hardly able to bear the quietness when it rattled to a stop.

There was a way to feel better, to fill the hole in his heart. A hole he'd created his own damn self. He picked up the phone and scrolled through the directory, not allowing himself to overthink what he was about to do. He was at a crossroad.

It was decision-making time.

By the river was where Lina missed Cole most.

This river, her childhood river, was nothing like the Thames. No lights sparkling off it when the man you loved held you in his arms, kissing you again and again.

A growl began to form in her chest, manifesting itself into a scream. *"No-o-o-o-o!"*

Her cry bounced back against the sheer stone edges shooting up from the opposite side of the river. Thank heavens her parents lived in the middle of nowhere. Here she had countless places to sneak away to, private nooks and crannies in the wilderness she'd escaped to as a child to dance in. And now she had returned, a grown woman, grieving the loss of the man who had captured her heart.

In the end she'd decided to treat her trip home as coming home. She'd finally plucked up the courage to ring Gemma and ask for her final boxes to be shipped home.

Home.

The word seemed even more weighted with meaning than ever before. Somehow, some way— in the space of three short months—home had become Cole Manning. His eyes, his smile, his skin, his touch. How a single thing in this small village in Poland could remind her of a doctor from America she didn't know. But it did.

The scent of the late summer flowers. Cole had given her flowers! Tucked one behind her ear the time he took her to Covent Garden. The coffee. Cole drank coffee! Thick and rich, just how she liked it. The *quiet*. The peaceful, sleepy quiet they enjoyed in his back garden that made the rest of London just slip away.

Really, she should be grateful. Grateful she'd only had three months' worth of her heart fall in love with him.

She threw three pebbles into the river. *Plop. Plop. Plop. Sink.*

Her shoulders slumped. Who was she kidding?

Her whole entire heart was his and her body was here in Poland, doing what exactly? Standing around with a fish she'd caught over half an hour ago for— She checked her watch. *Niebiosa!* She couldn't believe she'd lost track of time. She'd been doing a lot of that lately. It was nearly time for supper and she had the main dish!

As she ran, she did her best to let gratitude flood her body that she had so much. The ability to run without pain, the *energy* to run. Parents so loving she hadn't felt the slightest bit of shame when she'd finally told them everything—she had only felt comforted, loved. Her old fishing bag slapped against her thigh as she ran. She'd caught a beauty today. Her parents were in fits of giggles each time she brought one home.

"We haven't eaten some of these dishes in years, Michalina!" her father had crowed as she'd insisted on revisiting each of her childhood favorites. "We're not bumpkins, you know. Your mother makes excellent *risotto* and her *paella*? You'd think she was Spanish!"

But Lina had teased and cajoled and gone fishing, for hours on end, soaking up the sun and the meadow-grass-perfumed breeze, huge stacks of medical books by her side. Studying was the only thing that— Nope. Not even studying pushed Cole into the further reaches of her mind. Nothing could.

She ran through the garden and straight into the kitchen, where she was met by the sound of laughter.

There—flanked by her parents, with a cup of her mother's thick, black coffee in his hand and looking as relaxed and as comfortable as if he'd been there a hundred times—was Cole. The pile of boxes she'd left behind at the clinic was stacked neatly by the door. But she'd asked Gemma to ship—

Cole!

Her eyes darted from one parent to the other, their faces wreathed in delighted smiles, and then and only then did she let herself meet those sky-blue eyes that sent her belly on a giddy flip-flop butterfly tour.

What was he doing here?

To press his point home? To get her out of his life completely? To tell her he'd made a terrible mistake?

She could hear her parents commenting on the

traffic coming in from the airport, Cole's ability to travel light versus Lina's need for more, but none of it really registered. Her heart didn't even know what to do with the sheer volume of emotion she was experiencing.

Cole.

A warm heat spread through her chest. Watching his lips part into that knee-weakener of a smile felt like being warmed by a little slice of heaven.

She could hardly breathe.

In that moment Cole's eyes locked with hers. Anything that had felt incomplete in her life became whole. She loved him heart and soul. It was the most real thing she had ever felt.

"Earth to Lina." Cole's father waved a hand in front of her face. "Cole, you let this one run the front of your clinic? I am surprised given that she can't even offer you a kind greeting." Her father's voice was thick with pride.

"What are you doing here?" It was all she could manage. All she would allow herself.

"Lina!" her mother's tone was a chirpy chastisement. "Why, where are your manners?"

"Mamo, I'm not a little girl!" Lina was still staring into Cole's eyes, too focused to do little else.

If he was here just to rub her face in— *Stop! Give the man a chance.* Her voice softened. "What are you doing here?"

"Come, Marja." Lina's father shooed his wife away from Cole so he could get out from behind the table. "We are cramping the style of the young lovers."

Lina threw a mortified look at her father. Dads, it appeared, could still be embarrassing even when you were twenty-seven.

Cole took Lina's hand in his, tingly sparkles setting her body alight. Wasn't she meant to despise him? Her body certainly didn't. Or her smile.

"Want to show me around town?"

Town was about a hundred meters of a high street, if one were to call it that. It would only take about five minutes—if that. She tugged her hand free. It was still too much to process. She pulled her fishing tote off her shoulder and called to her mother, *"Mamo, będziemy mieć pierogi z rybą?"*

Cole's eyes ping-ponged between them, clearly hoping for a translation.

"I caught dinner!" She grinned, suddenly feeling as giddy as the teen she'd never really had the chance to be. "My mum is going to make my favorite dish from when I was a little girl."

Cole nodded, remembering. *"Pierogi."*

"Yes, good accent!" Lina's mother nodded, although it very clearly was not. How she could've doubted their kindness—their compassion—for even a second was beyond her. Lina pulled her mother into a quick squeeze before rejoining Cole at the door. "I love my mother." She beamed at her, dusty apron and all, from across the room. "You're a great mother, aren't you?" Her mother waved off the compliment, shooing them out the door as she did so.

Lina's mind did a quick recalculation. "Igor?" Her eyes shot to Cole, forehead raised in concern.

"Taken care of. Gemma has commandeered the full care and lavishing of affection he requires while I'm away."

"Is she the one...?"

"Who gave me your address? Yes."

"Go on." Lina's mother hustled them out of the kitchen, waving her kitchen towel at them to get out so she could have her domain left in peace.

Lina stood outside the house, looking around her. Were they having a joyful reunion or a horrid one? "Would you like to see the river?" If he was horrid, she could push him in. Just a little.

"I think somewhere private might be good." Cole gave her a wink.

"For what?"

"A talk." Cole looked serious and any giddy, excitement that had been playing round Lina's tummy collected in a dejected heap.

Ah.

They walked in silence until they reached the river's edge. She enjoyed his appreciative gaze as he took in what she thought was one of the most beautiful places in the world.

"You saved me, you know." He spoke the words to the river as if meeting her gaze would be too much.

"From what?" She sat on the sandy riverbank.

"Myself." He plunked himself down beside her, legs crossed, hands already busy pulling smooth river stones toward him.

"What do you mean?"

"I mean, you were there for me when I needed you." His gaze grew focused on the stones and he began to build a little tower.

"What are you talking about?" Lina drew back to inspect him. "I've been here."

"I rang my parents."

Lina's eyebrows shot up in surprise.

"I thought if you were brave enough to see your parents, I might follow suit."

"And?"

"Let's just say, I was wise to start with a phone call."

"Oh?"

"I won't be buying a ticket home—to North Carolina," he corrected, "for a while."

"I'm sorry." And she was. It had to have been a painful night and to have gone through it alone? It must've been awful.

He put on a brave face, picked up the stones one by one and flicked them across the river's smooth surface.

"Well, if I'm really honest. I can't say I expected anything less. So…after a bit of man time with Igor…"

Lina arched a curious eyebrow.

"I let him sleep on your pillow." Cole chuckled at the memory, the smile fading from his lips just as quickly. "Then I thought about everything else that was wrong with my life."

Lina folded her arms around her bent knees. She didn't know if she was ready to hear this. And how on earth had she saved him? And from what?

"All I wanted to do, Lina, was be with you."

Her eyes widened.

"I love you, Lina. I love you with all my heart. I think you're passionate. I think you're brave. I have hated every single moment you haven't been in London, in my—our—home, in my arms. I love you."

Lina blinked, staring into his eyes to see if what she saw there matched the words he'd just said. Was this really happening? He loved her?

"I can't believe you're here."

"I can't believe it took me this long."

They sat there a moment beside the river, each looking into the other's eyes until the tautness in their expressions softened. *They were together now.*

Lina scooped up handfuls of sand and scrubbed them along her bare feet, the intensity of emotion almost too much to bear.

"It's probably a good thing you decided to come

out here instead of using the telephone." Lina's tone slipped into dry humor mode. "With my non-changeable, nonrefundable ticket, having you here makes it much easier for me to get you to finally taste genuine Polish ice cream. It's beetroot season!"

Cole threw back his head and laughed. Laughed in way he hadn't since, well, since he and Lina had last been silly together. She had managed to bring that part of him back to life and he would be forever grateful to her.

"Marry me."

Her green eyes popped wide open, her mouth dropping into an astonished O.

"Study, work, whatever you want, but if you love me, please will you marry me? Come back to London. Come *home*," he said, only just resisting the urge to kiss her so that she could answer.

"Of course! Yes!" she answered, disbelief and happiness playing across her face. *"Yes!"* she shouted to the mountaintops soaring above them. *"Mam zamiar poślubić swoją miłoś!"*

"What are you saying, you beautiful woman?" Cole drew a hand through her hair, fingers teasing at the nape of her neck to come in closer, receive the kisses he so plainly had to give her.

"I am saying you have made me the happiest woman in the world." As his lips touched hers, Lina couldn't begin to believe this was only the beginning. The beginning of so many new things—all of them with Cole by her side.

"Shall we go tell your parents?" Cole's lips tickled along hers as he spoke. She stole another kiss before answering.

"Not just yet," she whispered, her lips meeting his again and again. "Not just yet."

* * * * *